AF269464

FATHER FIGURE

Also by Emma Forrest

FICTION

Namedropper
Thin Skin
Cherries in the Snow
Royals

NON-FICTION

Damage Control
Your Voice in My Head
Busy Being Free

FATHER FIGURE

Emma Forrest

WEIDENFELD & NICOLSON

First published in Great Britain in 2025 by Weidenfeld & Nicolson,
an imprint of The Orion Publishing Group Ltd
Carmelite House, 50 Victoria Embankment
London EC4Y ODZ

An Hachette UK Company

The authorised representative in the EEA is Hachette Ireland,
8 Castlecourt Centre, Dublin 15, D15 XTP3, Ireland (email: info@hbgi.ie)

1 3 5 7 9 10 8 6 4 2

A CIP catalogue record for this book is
available from the British Library.

ISBN (Hardback) 978 1 4746 2059 8
ISBN (Ebook) 978 1 4746 2061 1
ISBN (Audio) 978 1 3996 3390 1

Typeset by Born Group
Printed and bound in Great Britain by Clays Ltd, Elcograf S.p.A.

www.weidenfeldandnicolson.co.uk
www.orionbooks.co.uk

For Jenne Casarotto,
who signed me when I was sixteen.

'I will be your father figure
I have had enough of crime'

George Michael, 'Father Figure'

'Not everyone survives being rescued'

Adrian Nicole LeBlanc, Random Family

PROLOGUE

Ezra's comfortable middle age was tainted only by the knowledge that, in his heady youth, he had loved new wave music and killed people. The newspapers shared this knowledge but, due to British libel laws, could not print it. His past was audible only as a low accusatory hum when he entered a lunch meeting in a new space. Rumours oozed down the walls of gilded supper clubs like ectoplasm at a seance, all those whispered voices chanting as one to conjure ghosts he no longer believed in.

He lived a contented life with a woman he doted on, and a daughter who loved him. He worked each day to consolidate his business empire, at ease with himself because he had never brought harm to anyone he knew. He felt strongly that to hurt someone you are intimate with is a grave wickedness. It so offended his values that he kept lists of men he'd heard hurt wives or children – in an actual notebook in a special drawer of his St John's Wood mansion, which he'd go through from time to time to make sure it was up to date.

So, yes, back in the day, back in the old neighborhood, before he was middle aged and somewhat respectable – or, if not respectable, at least extremely charitable – he had arranged warning beatings and rarely – rarely! – outright hits. Once, an employee relayed to him how, in a particular instance of late payment, they'd extracted the money from the debtor by use of a hot whistle, heated over a stove, like they did in the real old East End. That had captured Ezra's interest as an amateur historian of the neighbourhood he'd grown up in, and where his elderly aunties still lived.

But the neighbourhood had changed and so had he. Imperative to his moral belief system: he'd never have done it himself with his own hands. For that you'd need far less control than he had. You'd have to have been awash with hormones that put you temporarily out of your mind, the way a teenage girl was.

PART 1

CHAPTER *1*

'I fellated a Cypriot fruiterer at the apex of Parliament Hill . . .'

As the headmistress read Gail's story to the sixteen-year-old's mother, Gail pre-empted her reaction, explaining, 'I think the flow of words really work for an opening line of a novel. *"Last night I dreamt I went to Manderley again."*'

The women both shifted in their metal chairs, as Gail repeated, clear and pleased with herself, in tones of Judi Dench: '"I fellated a Cypriot fruiterer at the apex of Parliament Hill." It wouldn't have the same rhythm if I had written "a Cypriot haberdasher". So you see what I was going for?'

Gail could, in her vivid imagination, already picture her as-yet unwritten novel launched at a literary festival, and knew that – though her readers really wanted to hear her work read in her own voice – this event was a kindness to Dame Judi who, in her head, was a fan. Maybe one of Gail's books had helped her navigate a bereavement, so it made sense to ask her to perform the reading.

But only moments after the daydream formed, Gail felt herself becoming resentful at how much Dame Judi had come to lean on her for support. Where once the legendary thespian's name on her imaginary caller ID had thrilled her, it now began to fill her with irritation, especially when the first thing Dame Judi always said in this fantasy when Gail picked up was 'It's only me!' Because who else would it fucking be? This festival reading was going to have to be their last hurrah together. She had huge respect for the woman, but Gail deserved a life too.

Deep in her daydream, Gail now had a look of thunder on her face so fearsome the headmistress and her mother – sat as far apart as the room would allow – could not help but look at each other for guidance. Coming back into her body, Gail was surprised to find herself sitting across from them, in the dark-wood office of an all-girls' school, the echo of slapped hockey pucks beyond the window.

The headmistress was so worried about mispronouncing Gail's mother's name that, though it was only three letters – Dar – she endeavoured never to say it out loud, her attempt at politeness rude. Dar noticed the headmistress was wearing a vintage Cartier Tank watch, slender and elegant. She thought it was the nicest thing about her. The worst was her voice, which was cheap gold plate: the class it was meant to indicate could easily be peeled off.

'Gail. Your English teacher brought me this essay. She found it, frankly, quite disturbing, especially on the first day of the new half-term.'

'Yes.' The girl nodded. 'I think it went over her head.'

Gail turned the offending pages on the desk to face her, and continued reading aloud: 'It was a very different fingering from days of youth, but then I am in my forties.'

Now Dar and the headmistress both looked at Gail but not at each other. She knew her mother had her at the semi-miraculous age of forty-three, was now fifty-nine, but she calculated her headmistress was probably in her mid-forties. Still, she forged ahead with her oratory: 'I had been divorced five years. I had gone on a few dates since then, but they were with appropriate people.'

Here Gail offered a footnote: 'It's obviously not *my* mother I'm writing about, as she doesn't date.'

Dar looked pleadingly at her to stop but did not have the nerve to speak out loud. This was notable as, in every context but Gail, Dar spoke with confidence and volume, the first to put up her hand (at work, in coffee shops, at any sign of an airport fracas). But Gail was her magic child and could do no wrong. Gail had filled a hole for her, but then kept digging. Dar knew in her heart of hearts they were now in a tunnel together and she prayed they would emerge onto a beautiful island at the other side. Only Gail had to be the one to dig the tunnel as Dar herself was very tired from being a single mother at such a late age. When she'd had the message to come in today, Dar was both weary because her workload at the hospital was too great and excited because she always liked talking about Gail.

Some of Dar's exhaustion was a result of her own choices, she freely admitted that. But there were other things freely her choice that she did not admit to, especially to herself. She'd been trying her best at life for a very long time, but the knowledge was encroaching that her best was not good enough – judging by the essay, her best wasn't even safe.

What wasn't clear was why the headmistress – who seemed in a trance – allowed Gail to keep reading. Gail projected her voice so it was louder than the din of the hockey game:

'I fellated him with the efficiency of a Sunday vacuuming, his beaming face the smooth carpet: a visible achievement, a small task whose completion makes you feel better about the day. They say, for mental health, you need to keep setting these small tasks . . .'

The headmistress leaned in to hear the payoff. She couldn't help it.

'. . . So I went back to the Heath the next day and did it again, but with a woman this time.'

This was finally too much for the headmistress, her sexuality a closely guarded secret, even from herself. She smacked her hands on her desk, hissing 'Stop!' – a sound that said her secret self had sprung a leak.

Gail looked at the headmistress slowly, as she imagined Dame Judi might were she to be interrupted on stage by the sound of a mobile phone. 'I did get in to this school on account of my creative writing, did I not?'

Did I not? The headmistress could see her parroting the words of the adults around her, saw her storing adult mannerisms in her pockets – one day they might get heavy and drown her. She wasn't sure if she'd be sad were this particular student to sink, never to be heard from again.

'Gail, this is . . . it's too creative. We'd like you to think just a little more inside the box.'

'I don't know if I'm able to. I don't know if I have that in me.'

The headmistress sat up straight. Dar finally tried to make eye contact with her but the headmistress would not meet her gaze, addressing only Gail:

'Then I don't know if St Saviour's is the right place for you. I think we shall have to keep this under review. It's May. We will allow you to complete the calendar year. But then we will make a decision before the Christmas break as to whether you'd be best off moving on in January.'

Dar finally spoke:

'Right. You're giving my daughter six months to prove what to you? And why? So the school can get one step closer to being completely homogenous?'

'You know that we embrace all cultures here!' The gold-plated voice of the headmistress was peeling, held under the cold tap of Dar's advocacy.

Dar squinted. 'I know the only Black student is the daughter of the Ghanaian Ambassador.'

The room was silenced by the mention of Faith. Even Gail herself went quiet.

The headmistress tucked a lock of dirty-blonde hair behind her reddening ear.

'I simply do not know that we are meant for each other. And if we are not, then it is best for both of us that we move on.' The implementation of school policy carried the weight of an ultimatum she'd never given nor would get to give to a lover. 'The school will come to a decision before we break for Christmas.'

'Well,' said Dar. 'Well, well.' As if she had been stewarding the conversation rather than dragged along by it, and was now guiding them to bring it to a genial close.

As they exited, Gail slamming the door behind her when she could just as easily have turned the doorknob to close it, the headmistress realised that the Susa women shared a scent. She imagined a flat with one bathroom, and a bottle of Dar's perfume whose use by Gail was sanctioned or prohibited. It was a metallic honey. She'd never smelled it before Gail arrived at the school. It was quite pretty when it was just one of them. But the two of them together in one small space made it hard to breathe.

All the girls in her year were at the age when they wanted to be picked up by men and then driven home by their mothers. When a girl was sent to the headmistress's office to discuss her behaviour, that was generally the subtext. None of them had expressed it as explicitly as Gail Susa.

Mother and daughter took the bus home, sitting on the top deck, at the very front, vying for the sacred spot with small children who wanted to pretend they were driving. They fought off the kids and settled in, averting their eyes from Parliament Hill as they passed it.

CHAPTER 2

Though they found solace on the upper deck, they were soon exiled downstairs because a pungent man was rambling noisily about Jews. Gail found the two often went together in London: unpleasant odour and public racism. She thought it uncommon to encounter a fragrant racist and unsettling since most of the notes in a pleasing scent come from foreign climes: Bulgarian rose, Persian saffron, Arabian oud.

Dar's Judaism was nothing she felt any shame about – her ethnicity was just something that grew from her without her consent and the way she saw it, the best thing she could do was attempt to style it like hair so it didn't obstruct her vision, pulling her Judaism coquettishly to the side, or parted centre to reveal more, or tied all the way back, no-nonsense, get things done.

Ever since university, she'd experienced Israel as a KICK ME sticker placed on her back. She'd shown up outside the embassy to protest the country every month, standing with 'The Jewish bloc'. This was her social life and where, last year, she'd befriended a Palestinian grad student who, like her, had green eyes and the benefit of 'passing'.

Her dad had done OK in England. He knew other Sephardim who fled Iraq, Morocco or Syria when he did who went on to become millionaires – he'd even met a half-billionaire. He himself rebuilt his life, working his way up until he owned a one-screen cinema. It gave Dar something that the other girls wanted and that helped her fit in at school, especially after her mother died.

Once he was gone, the only thing Dar wished she had was his watch, which had meant so much to him once upon a time. She wanted it on her bedside table at night, protecting her like an evil eye. She wanted to reach for it every morning and feel its cool weight on her wrist before she buckled the strap. Because, for reasons she'd yet to tell Gail, she didn't inherit it, and she noticed everyone else's. She didn't trust this generation because nobody wore watches and so she could not project onto them by dint of their accessories who they might be, and what they might want from her.

Dar's father never got to meet Gail, but they were connected by more than genetics: Dar's pregnancy was begat by grief for him. He looked like Gail, which made sense, but Dar spun it in her head as him looking down and protecting her. Gail had, like her grandpa, skin that went nut brown in the sun and then all the colour seeped out so they were pale in British winter. Dar's chin was pointy. Early on, she'd seen that chin in Gail and bitten it, like the final, best part of an ice-cream cone. But instead of the nub of chocolate you find there, she'd accidentally drawn blood. Maybe being an older mum didn't make her wiser, she was afraid in those days – what if it made her stupider? So she didn't try to *mother* mother. She decided she'd be better off being her best friend.

Both had curly black hair and an aquiline nose that Gail could either choose to make something great out of or 'fix', if she hadn't the moxie. Dar looked at her at eleven as her face started to change, features growing at different paces, and she knew she had the courage to keep it. This marked her out as different from most of her classmates, whatever school she was at – the visual difference and the embrace of the visual difference made her a figure of wariness.

She was the only girl at school who had no qualms about the features reflected back at her in the mirror, who'd sooner notice an issue with the mirror itself. One time, at a flea market, Gail, fresh with the first smattering of acne, stared deep into the mirror that had been set up to look into as you hold vintage clothes against your own outfit. Watching Gail fix on the glass, Dar thought, *Oh no, here it comes*, as her daughter stared and stared at the mirror, her features creased with criticism. Then she said, 'Mum?' And Dar steeled herself to affirm: 'You are perfect as you are! You are smart and strong and brave! You don't look like the other girls in class – you look like yourself!' And just as she was about to say it, Gail said what she'd intended to, which was: 'Mum, I much prefer rectangular mirrors to oval mirrors.'

Instinctively giving her the bus window seat as she'd instinctively given her the bigger bedroom in any flat they rented, Dar nudged her:

'I thought you would fight her for it? With all her sanctimony and repression? I was sure you were going to tell her how well you fit St Saviour's. I thought you really liked that school?'

Gail leaned her head on the glass. 'I *do* like it but I'm not going to beg a woman with such pale eyelashes, come on! They're damn lucky to have me there.'

She spoke as if she were not the only girl in her class on a financial bursary. She spoke as if she were not the only one in her class who lived in a high-rise flat instead of a house (they were not the only single-parent family – there was a woman who divorced well – but they were the only ones without child support). Dar had very much hoped to raise a daughter with high self-esteem, but maybe not as high as this.

Across the aisle from them on the lower deck, a small girl in overalls was sitting pressed against her mother. The girl watched, fascinated, as a young woman – Gail thought maybe aged twenty-three or twenty-four while Dar guessed eighteen – got on the bus carrying a rat. It was white with a long grey tail. It looked more impressive than the young woman who was holding it, her own skin and hair dull.

'Can I pet it?' shrieked the little girl, and both the girl's mother and the rat looked nervous.

Now everyone was interested in the young woman with dull skin and hair, who they'd not noticed, until they realised she was carrying something frightening – Gail stored this information.

'Please can I pet it?' the girl squealed. *How old are we when we start being scared of things?* thought Gail. She wasn't yet, but she felt right on the edge.

Because the rat was being transported by an owner on public transport, it was intriguing. But if it were in your home, if it were seen unexpectedly from the corner of your eye, you would scream and clutch your face.

Dar's mind got off at the wrong stop, and she found herself remembering being asked to feel the penis of a grown man when she was ten. He was in his early twenties, managing the music shop where she liked to touch the violins. She tried to be polite to him, as if there had merely been a confusion about what she wanted to touch. *This isn't the texture. This isn't the feeling.* She went home and told her dad, who, Dar following, stormed right out and punched the man in the shop. The shop soon had a new manager. That was the end of it. She wasn't blamed for anything and it was never mentioned again. The blessing and curse of a single dad instead of a single mother meant that danger was instantly dealt with but never discussed. Her mind came back to the bus, headed the right way, as she heard the young woman confirm:

'Yes, you can touch it,' the rodent crawling up her arm.

'No,' said the little girl's mother, sharply.

(Dar remembered the popping sound of her father's fist as it swung into the young man's jaw, how she'd checked to see if it was his fist or the man's cheek that had popped.) 'Ashkenazi scum,' her dad had hissed as he ran his bloody knuckles under the kitchen tap. So Dad had been both the one to win and the one to burst. She never saw inside him again. It was so startling, the inner mechanics of her father becoming momentarily visible to her, as startling, really, as the penis had been.

The bus rattled under an overpass. The mother and child got off at the next stop, the girl looking longingly back at the rat.

Dar nudged Gail and whispered, 'Did you see the kid's coat? So tacky to put a little girl in leopard print. You know what signal that gives the world about her?'

Gail sighed internally, not knowing what signal it gave the world, but not admitting her ignorance. What she *did* know was, no matter what she presented her with, her mother never noticed the right part in any picture.

CHAPTER 3

Processing the ultimatum the headmistress had handed her the day before, Gail got out her favourite pen, the one Dar had given her when she began at St Saviour's. It was a white-and-red checked print, like on a picnic blanket. She chose a rich purple ink, to indicate her deference to the letter's recipient.

Everyone who lived within the boroughs of Haringey, Camden and Islington and many of the denizens of Barnet knew George Michael's home address. Anyone who wanted to figure it out could figure it out. Gail hadn't even had to go looking for it. It had been revealed to her by the man who ran the corner shop, at the end of her first day as a sixth former at St Saviour's, without her asking or even having it on her mind.

She'd slouched in, a little lacklustre after scouting Faith – the ideal friend, popular, chatty, beautiful, an academic success – but failing to engage her in much chat. Gail's uniform felt stiff, like plastic, and chafed under her armpits where she'd recently begun shaving.

'Hello,' said the man behind the counter. 'First day back?'

'Yes,' she answered, warily.

All adult men are a bit creepy through the lens of a sixteen-year-old girl. It was sad, but she told herself at least she didn't have one in the house, like the girls with dads. She saw how uncomfortably they interacted with each other once the first swell of breast and body odour bloomed. Dar told her that where Grandpa had grown up, when he was a little boy, the Jewish girls had worn face veils when they hit puberty, just like the Muslim girls. Gail could see the appeal as she felt the shop keeper's eyes on her.

'How was it being back at school, then?' he prodded. He seemed, to her, to take pleasure in saying the word 'school'.

'I'm a bit shattered from it if you don't mind, and not really feeling like talking, I just want some chocolate.'

'Tsk tsk, I'll hush my mouth.' Now he seemed, to her, to take pleasure in saying the word 'mouth'.

His hushing up was unlikely, as just a few moments later he was leaning across the counter to say:

'You know he lives right near here?'

Before she could ask 'Who?' he pointed out George Michael on the cover of the *Evening Standard*. She bought a Wispa and took the free *Evening Standard* with the photo on the front page.

'Oh, yeah?'

'Yes, just across the street in Pond Square. It's the house with the black Range Rover parked outside.'

This was a lot of information for a first encounter. She'd wondered what he told people he actually knew. Was there any sliding scale of information provided? It wasn't framed as gossip, more like a local's orientation pack. She'd grasped immediately that the less response she gave the man, the more he offered her, and this was something else she filed away for later use on someone interesting.

'Good guy,' he'd said, nodding. 'Sweet guy. It's the house with the double-width chimney stacks.'

He couldn't share any more information than this without them sliding hand in hand down George Michael's chimney together, which might be physically possible because, as he said, it was double width.

Then he'd shaken his head. 'You never see him out any more.'

Instead of 'Because of people like you' she'd said, 'Oh.'

That's not right, she'd thought, *that's not right to give away the home address of such a private person*. But then he wasn't that private because he was on the cover of the paper for a sexual incident with a balding man at the back end of the Heath.

Gail understood, from navigating girls' schools, wanting to be left alone and wanting to lose yourself among a body of strangers. Her favourite place of isolation in any school she'd attended was always the school library – but she could also imagine having covert sex behind one of the shelves, and then walking away without saying anything. Not that she'd had sex before, but she could imagine it.

Walking past the butchers, she'd unwrapped her Wispa, upset at the man for revealing such personal detail, while simultaneously following his directions to go look. The man had been so disrespectful and so had the newspaper headline. She'd known right away: she wanted to help George Michael. If he wanted to have sex in public, he should feel free to, and she would let him know that. And if the sex in public was a cry for help, she would also help.

She spat out the Wispa, which had sat on the shop shelf too long in the heat. The chocolate was corrupted but the plan she began conjuring that day was pure. And that's how it began.

She was sealing her latest missive – her sixth in six months; she'd carefully restrained herself so as not to offer too much help all at once – when Dar trudged in from the hospital, the afternoon having slipped into the 'something more comfortable' of magic hour. She was carrying her top-handle handbag in one hand and a plastic bag from Budgens in the other. It annoyed her daughter that she carried a doctor's-style bag even though she was a nurse. It seemed like a constant public complaint – that, because of her gender or maybe her ethnicity, she had not been fully rewarded. It implied a desire to be asked what she did – 'I couldn't help but notice your bag! Are you a doctor?' 'No I'm a nurse!' Or simpler, since the bag was designed in such a way that it could not be slung over her shoulder, it gave a constant excuse for her to say, 'I have no hands free. I need a hand.' And the only person ever there to lend her mother a hand was Gail. She might have said to Dar as she entered with her bag, 'Is there a doctor in the house?' in tones of mock emergency. But teasing always implied a desire to get closer. So she kept it to herself.

As Dar unpacked the Budgens carrier bag piece by piece, fish fingers in the freezer and fresh fruit in the crisping drawer, Gail stood beside her until Dar asked, 'Are you going to help me?' Gail stretched her arms over her head and yawned. 'I've just written quite a long letter to George Michael.' She had the same tone as when she'd announced, 'I've moved all my money to the Bank of Shanghai,' when what she'd meant was that she'd transferred her beginners' savings account from NatWest to HSBC. Point being, she had undertaken a great, exhausting effort and that was the only reason she'd not offered to help unpack. Dar responded suitably, with a non-committal:

'Lovely!'

'Lovely?' Gail replied, icy.

Dar forged ahead – she always tried to forge ahead so that these moments could become parades instead of protests: 'Yes. I think it's great that you write to him. It's nice to put things down on paper, hardly anyone does that any more.'

She wondered if Gail's fascination with a pop star from her youth was connected to their intense closeness. It was flattering.

'And writing to him has probably helped you figure out a lot.'

'No. It hasn't.'

'Oh,' she continued, her torrent of words in the face of Gail's reticence equivalent to being a close talker, 'because I know that meeting yesterday was hard. It sucks to have this hanging over your head.'

'It wasn't hard,' Gail said curtly, Dar's endless *understanding* on her skin like hot breath.

'. . . And even though the school are so lucky to have you, and she has no right to make you feel like you're on trial, or you have something to prove to her, I thought you could figure out what's been bothering you. And then maybe keep it for yourself instead of posting it to George Michael. Or instead of having to freak out the school with sexualised essays? I mean, you can always just talk to me.'

'Why? He's the one I'm trying to help.' Her teeth were perfect, framed by a curled lip. 'This isn't about me. Don't let the school live rent-free in your head.'

Dar counted the amount she'd spent on Gail's orthodontics – 2K? 3K in the end with the times she replaced her lost night guard. 'Well . . . it's not free. I do pay for it. Even on a reduced scale.'

'I thought the most important thing in life was to be myself?'

Dar tried to stay upbeat – her internal mantra 'parade not protest, parade not protest'. 'I mean . . . it's a great quality, but I'm not sure it's *the* most important thing?'

'Fuck's sake!' (Gail didn't like saying 'fuck' unless it was in front of Dar, whose presence was like an overpass lending rude words a pleasing echo.)

'Gail, I'm very tired.' She felt it deeply enough in her joints that she knew there was no benefit to looking in the mirror when she brushed her teeth tonight. If she'd slept and eaten well, if she hadn't drunk anything, she looked lovely. When she'd had a bad night's sleep and a rough day at work, her reflection showed her face speeding towards the end like a flip book.

'You're always tired! Maybe you were too tired to see how powerful my story was. How ahead of my years it is.'

'Maybe you're right.' Dar had tried this same tone with her lover as he was leaving – Gail, as if by osmosis, had begun writing letters to George Michael at the same moment Dar had wanted to pepper her ex with pleading missives. Instead, she'd quietly intoned, 'I understand, I understand,' even as she flailed inside.

'Well. That's very disappointing,' Gail concluded. She didn't like it when her mother acquiesced, which was several times a day.

'Gail, you try being a mother of a teenage girl when you're almost sixty!'

'No, thanks! I think it's a horrid idea!' Gail had picked up 'horrid' as a child from reading Enid Blyton, and Dar had to chew her lips not to laugh each time she said it. Today she was too exhausted to laugh, to chew or to fight.

Dar was baked, over-baked even, whereas Gail hadn't finished being cooked yet. Risky as it was to open the oven door, things could still be added to Gail's mixture, even if there was no guarantee the ingredients would mix. It could all fall apart. But it could still be *tried*.

Finally, in an attempt to re-set the conversation, Dar accidentally blew it up. 'You deserve to stay at the school. But I also understand if maybe you've been pushing their buttons because there's a part of you that would like to get a fresh start somewhere, away from Faith.'

CHAPTER *4*

Gail wasn't hungry for dinner that night, and she didn't want to watch TV or go to bed. So she decided to post the letter instead of waiting for morning. She stormed out of their building, intending to take the envelope to the post box at the end of their street.

But this time, she was so angry with Dar, the anger powered her to keep walking, and then further still, past Fortis Green, down Muswell Hill Road, all the way to Highgate village. The cold evening sky and birds having evening chats where they rounded up the day's events kept her pace steady.

There was an implicit understanding that Dar was not ever to mention Faith. But she was getting older and more forgetful. After a day at work she often had the boundaries of water. And so she had conjured she who must not be spoken of, right in their kitchen, with shopping on the counter and the walls closing in.

With each stride, Gail tried to step outside the memory of how it had gone wrong. How they'd been dawdling at the gates after school and Gail asked Faith if she wanted to see where George Michael lived. How Faith made a face

– an ugly expression on a pretty face, so utterly compelling to Gail! – and suggested they go for coffee and a gossip. But what did they have to gossip about? What did either of them have to put on the table and decimate that was actually of value?

Still, she went with her. It meant something that there was a coffee shop with Gail's name on it. All over the city, increasingly so, growing, like her confidence. Was she feeling more powerful lately because her name was everywhere or was her name everywhere because of her increasing power?

'Kismet!' she said to Faith as her name loomed, red on white, above the store front. 'Yeah, maybe?' Faith only half agreed. They sat in their uniforms, Faith's skirt hiked high, Gail's tailored low, picking at matching cookies.

When all the crumbs had been pressed into Gail's mouth, she traced her finger on the blemish-free porcelain. 'What are you interested in?' She rephrased it in a young person's voice: 'What are you into?' But that was the problem, and it had been a problem for Gail before at previous schools and would be again – Faith didn't know what she was interested in, given that she was only very young.

Girls who were perfectly placed and happy at a school still changed to somewhere new for sixth form, because it might lead to something new happening, which might lead to them knowing what they were into. Others moved because they knew exactly what they were into and their dogged pursuit of it led to things going awry at school. That's how Gail had arrived at St Saviour's, though her mother would never have pitched it that way.

Gail touched Faith's elbow with her elbow, mentally prepping to touch her knee with her knee, and said, 'I'm going to be a writer so why don't we have a book club?'

Gail took out a pen and made a list of novels and memoirs they could explore. Faith wasn't dumb – she was academically succeeding far beyond Gail. But she looked at the list and said she did not wish to read the collected works of Solzhenitsyn. Gail pushed this feeling aside that they were perhaps not an ideal match, because with that would come the fear, one school on, that there might be no match for her out there. And that would leave her back where she started, her and her mother.

She asked her to just give it a go, and stopped at the Highgate book shop, paying for both copies of each book choice herself. Then they stopped at the creepy grocer and, with snacks in tow, headed off to the Heath. But she noticed, soon, Faith looking away from her when there were boys nearby and felt she was even sitting deliberately too far away, so their conversation did not quite reach each other. She had the sense that she was holding out a joke to Faith on the end of a long stick to try to bridge the space.

'Rah! She got legs, man!' One boy cried as Faith stretched her legs in front of her. Gail stood up and stepped forward in her very long skirt and said to the boy, who could only have been two years older than them, 'Obviously she has legs. I mean, obviously.'

Faith was terribly embarrassed by her response and stood up and walked on ahead, leaving behind her new book.

When, lugging their stuff, she caught up with her, Gail argued: 'But, Faith, what he said was stupid. It made no literal or allegorical sense.'

Faith spun around.

'Oh my God! He was just trying to get me to pay him attention!'

Gail paused.

'Why would you pay attention to him?'

Faith spun on her heel, walked back to where they'd been and sat down with the leering boys.

'What are you doing, Faith?'

'Go away.'

But Gail didn't go away, she stood her ground. Faith would never, with her looks, have to pretend that she did like anything she didn't. That was how Gail, through her devotion to beauty, saw it. That's why she was all the more disappointed when she watched Faith crumble in the presence of a boy.

Realising Gail was not going to leave, Faith went into the bushes with the boy in order to have some space, even if, once his finger had reached up her skirt, under her knickers and found its way inside her, she really had less space. It was such a strange, unpleasant feeling; it fused with how overbearing Gail had become over six weeks of friendship. She focused her disgust on Gail and they never really spoke again.

Many St Saviour's girls go cottaging in the park after school, like George Michael when he was caught here, or not far off, for they hang around bushes hoping to kiss boys they don't yet know. What Faith did to get Gail to leave her alone was hardly out of the ordinary. A St Saviour's girl just did it, usually, for a more banal reason, rarely to do with desire, mainly to do with attention.

But, for Gail, the shame of the failed friendship remained so intense, she'd find herself getting high off it. She was surprised, having fallen into this bad memory, to find herself back in the here and now, the heavy cream envelope in her hand.

It always felt like following a ley line, walking to George's. Even if the man hadn't told her, months ago, which house it was, the house drew you. The central square with its patch of green grass at its core. You couldn't lie on it, but you could look at it. Something quite distinct from the Heath and only for the wealthy – look but don't touch, for your eyes only. It took more imagination than a garden square with a residents-only key, but she could see the payoff.

So that, when she was finally there, she was removed from the intimidation of it being *his* house, with possibly *him* inside it. The first time she'd stood outside, she'd doubted herself. These little windows of insight that she might not be doing the right thing, that she might not be in control, that she was only sixteen years old, frightened her and the next day she would awaken as if from a fever, having sweated the insight out of her skin like an illness to be overcome.

But Dar had transgressed by saying Faith's name out loud. So she was going to transgress today, too. She looked around. There was no visible security, this or any other night. 'Do it,' she said to herself, and then out loud, 'Do it.' A bird made its final call of the evening: it wasn't even speaking to her, but she took it as a sign. She stepped forward, and then again. No volume control on her pep talk, she slammed the envelope through the gilded letterbox with such a flourish that, even a hall removed, the pop star's dogs were interrupted in their sleep.

The dogs were one way people in the neighbourhood might get lucky enough to see him. They had to be walked and sometimes it had to be by him. There were very famous people in the world who had tiny little dogs so they wouldn't have to go outside their front door. But that wasn't what George Michael had chosen as pets. He'd have liked to stay inside, but they needed their freedom, just as much as he needed his privacy. Walking the two yellow labradors, he acted out the tug of his own greatest songs, craving solitude but needing to be in the world.

She had sealed the missive, but she knew it off by heart, could recite it like the French homework she hadn't done:

Dear George,

I read you said you only cottage on Hampstead Heath when it's warm enough and I wanted to say, I do understand that logic, since hot places are in our blood. I don't think you'll object to me bringing this up in a fan letter since you brought it up in an interview and the writer didn't even seem like much of a fan. You're just too open. But then that probably does help with the cottaging.

Can I ask some questions that you're not obliged to answer? What exactly happens in cottaging? Are there different symbols for each particular act? Can you say 'stop' once you've started something? Can you say 'I wanted to do that but now I don't want to do that'? Like reaching a new patch of the same sea where the temperature changes and you want to get out right away? That's the main thing I wonder about sex and why I haven't tried it even though I'm sixteen. Is it

OK to have some of it but not all of it? Or once I start having sex am I going to be obliged to forge ahead with it all, forever? Is it more like an 'on/off' switch? This isn't for my real life, George, it's for something I've been thinking of writing.

George, I hope you won't mind me saying, but it is extremely confusing in the 'I Want Your Sex' video when you're singing right into the model's ear and she just stares straight ahead. It makes it seem like you are trying to fuck a deaf woman. I hope that's OK to say. George, it looks like you really do not want to have sex with her even though you're saying that you do. As a teenage girl, I relate to that. If the girls in my class would ever admit it, they'd say the same.

So anyway, I understand what you've been through the last few years and I'd like to help, and I think that I can. There's a reason you could rely on Andrew Ridgeley from the first day you showed up in his class. He was Egyptian, you were Greek, you guys were the same but different, that's what made Wham! battle-proof. This is in my blood, too. These English people, they aren't like us and we aren't like them. If you're not talking to Andrew (and maybe you are?) but if you aren't talking to him at the moment, because you've grown apart or whatever, maybe you need a new ear. An ear that's the same but different. In which case, you can always talk to me. I am a great listener. I have listened to my mother all my life.

Your Friend,
Gail Susa

She was tired, from walking all that way, from going over the painful memories of the betrayal by Faith, from having her stupid mother as a mother, from doing what she just did. So, overwhelmed by it all, she ordered an Uber home, which collected her promptly before charging her stupid mother's dumb credit card.

Waiting in the darkening flat, Dar had been wondering for some time when Gail's feelings for Faith, obviously unreciprocated, would come to a head. They had been here before. It was not something she could protest: to signpost it would make things far worse between them. Her phone pinged with the Uber notification and she could keep track of Gail – electronically, could follow the places she'd been, the paths she'd taken. But there were back streets of Gail's heart she'd never know. Living in the era where mothers could track their children digitally only made her daughter's emotional secrecy more challenging to accept. She could not see what she could not see. And Gail could not have what she could not have.

CHAPTER 5

Over a Saturday-morning breakfast of cinnamon bagels, Dar said, 'I'm sorry I'm always so tired.'

Gail picked a raisin out and turned to face her.

'No, I'm sorry.'

Dar's heart expanded like a bubble-gum balloon blown to its limit by an exceptionally bold child. 'Are you?'

'Not really.'

Pop!

'OK,' agreed Dar, covering her disappointment, feeling in the dark for the same gently sarcastic wavelength. 'Neither am I.'

And they hugged and watched TV on the sofa. Even though every third channel they passed had the football on, they were pleased for each other's warmth.

'Be afraid of British football fans,' Dar said, darkly. 'Be afraid of them if their team wins and be afraid of them if they lose.'

Dar had intense, lateral anxieties. 'Can you hold that slice of pizza a bit more carefully, please?' she once asked Gail, concerned that she might poke her own eye with the pointed end. Where did it all come from, the fear she cocooned her daughter with, as if it were love? Sometimes she couldn't help but press into her mother's fears as a way to stay seen.

Gail sometimes put her hand in her mother's hair and turned the ringlets with her fingers, as a parent does to a child. It was the only time Dar would hold out a beat before murmuring, 'Hey, can you stop that?' and try to move away. She didn't like the roles reversing.

Dar thought she lived a life of selfless need to give her daughter the life *she* deserved. And her daughter thought at every turn, *I deserve so much more than this*. But what were the other things she deserved? She wasn't yet sure of this – in this respect she was very much only sixteen. And so the want grew larger, diffused only by an attachment to a local pop star or to Faith while it lasted, sometimes to an item of clothing or a gesture in a film.

Gail had looked at her mother and the way their faces were alike. She'd hated the smell of Dar's perfume, and then one day come to like it, like the day you taste coffee and the bitterness feeds you. The thing she'd not herself noted was: she started wanting to share her scent around the same time she began wanting to get away. Writing would do it, too. In her head, she imagined her mother very proud though she rarely imagined her at her book events.

She'd dedicate her first book to her. Obviously! To her mother and to George, and she'd decide right before it went to the printers which order they should fall in. George needed her help. She felt pretty sure there was nothing more she could give her mother.

Her mother was her horizon, endless, frightening,

comforting, unknowable, but still the point she always focused on to stay steady and to dream into, and she was, when she gazed out at her, the great well of emptiness. Because there was no father. She didn't need a shrink to tell her that, but she'd still been sent to one from the age of nine, until funds ran low and then they didn't speak of it again – the need for the psychiatry nor the low funds.

'Ashkenazi and their fucking psychiatry! They'd all be fine if they'd have a drink now and then.' (Dar heard her father's voice when she said this, how he'd move between Arabic and Hebrew, a Middle Eastern Spanglish.) Then she'd nod and add, 'I'm allowed to say that because I'm Jewish.' Dar was particularly suspicious of Hassidim, moving away from them on Underground platforms, booking flights that took off on Saturdays so she'd know for sure she'd never have to sit next to them. Gail had wondered for many years now just how terrible a thing you might be allowed to say about a group of people if you were one of them. And more nagging than that: if you said a terrible enough thing about your own people, might you become something else?

'But we're not *like them*,' reasoned Dar. But that's what Gail said to herself about her classmates and all it got her was being alone and confused. The football fans, she admired this about them: the group chanting, the recognition that the one who is visibly identifiable as not like you could potentially harm you. But the swarm and sound of them, any fan in any team's colours, alarmed her, just as her mother crossed the street from the Hassids in their black hats.

She hated the sound of them as she emerged from an Underground station. All those men in the same scarves, emboldened by use of colour theory to group joy or violence. Drinking as much as they could as fast as they could. The bodies in the streets the next day – not death, just drunkenness. How the tabloids and their readers laughed when it was a royal child or the son of a prime minister found splayed on the pavement. A rite of passage to be blackout drunk. It wasn't safe, she thought.

The sound of the lift coming up and down while they were watching TV had maybe once, long ago, irritated them, but by this point it had become comforting, rhythmic. When they could not hear the lift, they knew they'd be carrying the Budgens shop up and down the five flights. That Dar would pause and catch her breath and talk about her bad knees and her age, and Gail would feel both disdainful and extremely frightened at the notion of a life after her mother.

Beyond the sitting area, the view from their top-floor flat was incredible, and offered hope that, despite not being wealthy, they could see things that other people couldn't. They could spot far-off danger and cut big egos down to size with their perspective.

Dar knew they were going the wrong way. The third-floor flat. Then the higher flat. You'd think it was an ascent, to go higher. But she knew it wasn't. Gail didn't think it was. She could see it tracked with Dar seeming sadder and more tired. But Gail did love being able to see all across the park, when they were moved here.

On the first and last time she'd brought Faith to the flat, Gail had watched as Faith took in the small rooms. Gail understood: they were meant to be rich. She'd often looked from room to room of the flat, thinking the same thing. Gail could have explained, as her mother had to her: my grandfather had to leave all that behind when he was forced to leave Iraq. We never managed to figure out a way to get it back.

She was envious of Faith's healthy beauty, the bright whiteness of her teeth, the gleam of her skin, the muscle tone she wielded in hockey and that day she'd been here, just laying on the sofa. She was amazed that she put her feet up on the sofa in her shoes, in another person's house!

On the way down, the lift hadn't worked and they'd had to walk the flights of stairs, each landing offering secret shadows to kiss her in or push her down. Her mother once said to engage your core more carefully when you're going downhill than up if you want to protect your back and Gail hated that she was thinking, besides sex and death, of her mother and her mother's back pain.

Sometimes she worried that there must be tales about their flat going round school since the breakup with Faith – how small and cramped it was.

But, if that was what Faith was telling the girls, Gail knew in her heart she was wrong and that their flat was special. Faith hadn't noticed the brass panel on the bathroom door, inlaid with an art nouveau floral motif, or the hearts moulded into the iron of the fireplace; she didn't see the shiny green tile. The wood carved into the wall that was inset with a mirror and the wood itself inlaid with fans. The plaster cornicing around the ceiling. All the details you could find in a rich person's house, all the things they'd point out in a four-million-pound mansion. Just tiny. And high up. Because, back in the day, that level of decoration was also permitted for people who weren't wealthy, that it might 'improve' them.

Dar flicked past the football match again and touched her daughter's toe with her toe. 'So where were you all that time last night when you were raging at me?'

'I went to the soda counter,' Gail said, which her mother accepted as fact, though no soda fountain had ever been mentioned, not by her daughter or anyone else in the United Kingdom. Gail knew in her gut it was an odd lie, since she'd not done anything wrong, not stolen or graffitied or hurt anyone. She'd posted a letter through a troubled pop star's letterbox. Was it a transgression? Depended who you asked. She knew, maybe, she was just practising the shape of lies so the muscle would be lubricated when she one day needed to sprint. For now she sank deeper into the sofa and held her mother's hand, whose neat manicure offset its lines on olive skin.

'Why is the fucking football on every fucking channel?' Gail grumbled.

'Even I know this is a big one,' Dar laughed.

'Why?'

'Because of who bought the team.'

But Gail had already zoned out.

CHAPTER 6

For someone so often described as shameless, Ezra Levy had several acute sources of embarrassment. In his fiftieth year, he thought one of the most humiliating things you could do was to use the St John's Wood Beatles crossing to actually cross the road. Since he lived in St John's Wood, two streets from the Abbey Road Studios, this was an issue never far from his mind. He admitted (to himself, since he was the only one who knew of this phobia) that one could, with forethought and self-loathing, plan a more humiliating event. But this was by far the most humiliating situation Ezra occasionally found himself wandering into, while going about his domestic life. He was, as the papers made clear, a vulgarian (a more generous reading by the few who loved him was that he was a bold and exuberant man, right down to his thundering footsteps). The feeling it had given him, the times it *had* accidentally happened, when he had wandered into the sea of tourists as they timed their photos – together, apart, together, apart – had punctured his joie de vivre to such an extent that he felt haunted by it. He thought of it in business meetings and once on the phone to Vladimir Putin and another time while unveiling a bedding collaboration with Kate Moss. He had leaned on the staged bed frame, feeling sick.

Ezra was generally in his limo, but he loved his neighbourhood, was still delighted he'd made it from the East End to the north, which though technically diagonal was clearly upwards, and he liked to walk. Especially on bluesky days, to the newsagent, or the flower stall, the deli and the hospital when there had been the worst weeks of what he and his wife called *the great unpleasantness*. He would always try to make sure he'd crossed the road well before he needed to. The one or two times he'd been caught – it wasn't just about being recognised, the occasional savvy Londoner turning a lens on him. It was that the repurposing had changed the crossing forever, tourists literally stopping traffic to shoot their shot. A family of four visitors celebrating Britain at the height of its global glamour, working in sync to make a holiday card that would surprise and delight everyone on their Christmas list all across the world. Ezra didn't judge them for this. He had done it, too – zeroed in on the Greatness of Britain at particular moments in time, going so far as to say his birthday was the same as Winston Churchill's, and having a swinging sixties party for his last birthday. He didn't judge the tourists, he just didn't want to get involved. Stop, gap, pause, try with pleading eyes not to get hit. It was needy of them. Neediness is the worst.

Some of the refugees from Russia who made up his family tree found refuge in England instead of America and that's why they said zebra not zeebra, Levy not Leevy. Yes, the zebra crossing was there. Yes, cars were still obliged to stop for its intended purpose. But that wasn't what it meant any more, not on this corner outside this recording studio, and if you used it as it was first intended to be used, could it be two things at once, the functional and the fantasy? Can it be what it was first intended to be if you're stepping, purposeful, into other people's photos and seeping into their dreams?

One time he walked into it by mistake because he was thinking about his football team, the one he supported so devoutly that he'd gone ahead and bought them.

One time he was fixating on the department store he'd been blocked from owning.

One time he was thinking about the only family member who had truly caused him suffering.

As the weeks passed, Faith grew tighter with her new social huddle, lacing them to her. Gail was on her own, by the few outsiders. *By*, not *with*, the outsiders, since the outsiders did not have the social skills to come together, only orbiting each other like satellites. Gail's long, narrow skirt isolating her more, so even if there had been girls she wanted to be with, she'd not have been able to keep up.

How painful it is, knowing to your bones that you are a major planet but the universe is saying you've been downgraded to merely a dwarf planet. Painful but *motivating*. How can you punish them for the way they have diminished you?

Then, one day, a new student arrived.

PART 2

CHAPTER 7

Rushing to beat the bell, curtailed by her long, narrow skirt, the first thing Gail had spotted in the early June sunshine was the ramp that had appeared overnight.

As she rounded the corner, a girl was being pushed up the corridor in a wheelchair. At St Saviour's, the more space you took up at school, the less you were looked at. So if you were extremely fat, you'd not get a look-in. Likewise, though she was a new girl *and* late-term arrival, both of which would have made her of interest to the other pupils, the fact that she was in a large and unwieldy, bright silver wheelchair made her absolutely invisible. Gail *was* interested, and she smiled when she passed the girl outside the library, to show her empathy. It was hard to gauge the new girl's response, as her face was pinched with discomfort.

The wheels themselves were silent, top of the range, gliding like a skater on ice. If she'd been in better shape, the girl could have pushed it herself, but her arms were too weak, withered. The only sound came from the male healthcare worker who was pushing her. He was a decent-enough looking man, he had a pleasant face, a full head of hair and all his own teeth – but in the context of the all-girls' school he became spectacular.

For the rest of the day, the girls listened for the sound of his feet on the linoleum as if it were an ice-cream-van jingle. They waited behind corners, watching the muscles ripple in his arms as he guided her where she needed to go. Only Gail came alive at how the girl put all her trust in him, because she had to. Only Gail thought how much she would give to be the one a wheelchair-bound girl trusts.

They had not thought through – the parents of the girl, nor the school – what would be unleashed if you were to assign a child a male nurse at an all-girls' school. And under thirty years old. On him, all eyes fell.

'How old do you reckon he is?' she heard Faith say. She jumped in with an answer even as Faith turned away:

'Well, nurses are very badly paid. If he were over thirty and being paid that little, could you get hard for him?'

Gail liked to say she could or couldn't 'get hard', though she did not have a penis and, unlike many girls in class, had never seen one before. She did not imagine it *hard* both in blood flow and to navigate, only that it conferred power. She had little of that, as yet. She hoped to gain power, as ever, by showing how little she cared about having any. It had never worked before and yet she pressed doggedly ahead.

Despite the fact that he was only there to wheel the girl, they stared at him, each of them, imagining different things: him leaning against a locker at the end of the day, eyes half closed with exhaustion, or was it longing? His arms that pushed the wheelchair, holding a door open for them, then, maybe, pushing them to the ground. So invested were they in their fantasies about the male nurse that they had allotted no time at all to figure out who the girl was. They approached the pair in the corridors that first day as if, rather than he being the one pushing her, she were an appendage pulling him through the halls for their pleasure.

The toilets – the VIP room of school – were a-chatter by lunchtime. If you really needed to use them for their given purpose, you were out of luck that day. 'Try later,' the overwatered were told, the ones who'd foolishly skipped and jumped at breaktime and then used the drinking fountain, as girls hogged the stalls to verbally fantasise about the man, one bold girl locking herself in and quietly rubbing one out.

'I would climb him like a drainpipe,' Faith suddenly said. The girls she'd begun associating with laughed and clapped their hands and agreed, and so Faith kept going: 'I would climb him like a drainpipe so fast, he wouldn't know what had hit him.' But then, over the throng of girls, she caught Gail's eye, and looked down and stopped talking and quickly turned her back. Gail said nothing, only thought inwardly, *Why? Why would you climb the drainpipe? Why is the drainpipe there? It is dangerous. Someone could get into your bedroom. Somebody could hurt you. You could fall. You could die or live but be laughed at. You'd let yourself be climbed but you're too scared to climb anyone and we both know it.*

They all went home chattering about him. Past the gates, up the street, some to the Overground, some to the bus stops, the lucky ones to taxis or waiting cars. A few, like Gail, who usually resented walking, today wanted to walk home, so they could carry the thought of him with them. Only she knew in a way the others didn't that she was attuned to him just because he was the only man in her field of vision. She could see, could feel, how small he felt in the world.

They were all so taken up, they didn't see the male nurse as he wheeled the new girl down the specially made ramp. To the waiting car. How he helped her in, past the smoked-glass window, to someone waiting inside it, before he himself went on his way, to his domestic happiness with his chef boyfriend in a one-bed Peabody-estate flat they'd saved for in Kennington, leaving the girl in her wheelchair to her enormous wealth and privilege and diminished health.

It took the parents to alert the schoolgirls. And even that took a beat because nothing they were interested in was interesting to their teenage daughters. But their fizzing, anxious gossip in the guise of deep concern was impossible to miss even to narcissistic sixteen-year-olds. They finally noted their parents behaving like teenage girls – WhatsApping on the group chat and in illegal splinter groups about who the new arrival really was. Some parents were very excited and made love that night after lengthy dry spells. The girls had not seen their parents thrilled like that. Then *they* began to text each other.

Dar, and Dar alone, was in an absolute rage, worse than any incident Gail had ever seen involving her mother at any of the schools she'd attended. If you didn't know better you'd say Dar was aroused as she cried:

'Do you know who this new girl's father is? Do you know who her father is?'

And Gail was nervous and aroused, and she did not know who this girl's father was.

CHAPTER 8

Gail met England's most powerful nefarious force on a day he happened to be feeling pretty vulnerable. Though he understood he had power – the chauffeur and bodyguard and beautiful second wife who came from a country that had murdered his recent ancestors confirmed that in his own narrowed eyes as well as the wider world's – he, of course, did not see himself as nefarious. And, every ten years, Ezra would, as any normal, non-nefarious man might, think: *This beard and moustache make me look too forbidding!* And he'd shave off his beard and moustache – usually when the sun came out and his skin felt itchy and hot. Every time, he discovered as if it were new information that without his facial accoutrements, he looked like a Semitic Björn from ABBA. He did it over and over, without fail, each decade, opening and closing the fridge door to find the bare, empty shelf that was his own nose-to-lip ratio. He would have to lay low so the tabloids didn't capture this.

He'd have to lie low for two weeks. Two weeks lying low meant a lot of time with his wife and daughter. That's how it started. That's how he started breaking off his office hours to collect Agata from her new school. If he hadn't screwed up by the minor disaster of shaving, the major disaster might not have happened.

When he came downstairs at breakfast, everyone in his orbit pretended nothing was different. Not even his own wife acknowledged the very visible mistake. Agata tilted her head away, though her wheelchair remained forward facing. Their wilful disengagement left him feeling as empty as his upper lip. He slumped down in his chair as the chef brought him his grapefruit juice: even with his decades of wealth and power he could make the same mistake as any other Englishman in a heatwave.

But he wasn't English, was he? Not really. Not to *them*. Or they'd have let him have his department store. 'Them' was always the papers, always, but usually also the cabinets of both political parties and often fellow diners in his Mayfair members' club. Once 'them' had included his former father-in-law, though he wasn't considered properly English either. A few years ago he added to 'them' a middle-aged cashier he'd crossed paths with at the late-night Marks & Spencer in St Pancras station after disembarking the Eurostar, but he then rescinded this on realising the man simply had a wall eye. Ezra had, as penance, had an assistant go back and offer the cashier a high-paying job. The cashier was confused. If he'd ever checked up on him, Ezra would have found that the man had, on his new wages, been able to pay for his elderly mother to enter the best private care home and that every Sunday when he visited her, they toasted Ezra's greatness, even as her dementia progressed and she wasn't certain who she was toasting.

To cross Ezra's bad side and then be redeemed, the rare acknowledgement of a mistake on his part, had boosted several lives and made a few careers. There were, as previously mentioned, also several people dead who had not only *not* been redeemed but had fallen further foul. As much as they'd bothered him while alive, he never really thought of them once they were gone. Delegate, delegate, delegate. He had a wife, a tailor, a housekeeper, a chef, a bodyguard and a 'fixer'.

The shaving mistake, however, just like the accidental use of the Abbey Road zebra crossing, was always derailing.

He'd thought, beyond feeling too hot, that perhaps the moustache was too swarthy, that it emphasised the desert DNA they alluded to in the subtext and *text* of their critiques. They'd let him buy a football club, fine, because that's just poor people's culture. And, before that, a tabloid TV channel – that's poor person stuff, too. And at the start, a chain store selling clothes made in the kind of factories his forebears had once worked. But not the most storied and beautiful department store in the UK, woven into the very history of London society. Again and again *they* stood in his path, like the tourists standing gormless on the glorious building's gilded escalators. So maybe the answer was under the facial hair. The moustache was just too Omar Sharif. The beard too Rabbinic. But underneath his skin was olive. And would go more so now the sun was out and the beard was off. And you could see. You could just see – if you were looking for it – that he wasn't from round here. And people *were* looking for it.

The more he wanted this one ridiculous thing, the more they said he couldn't have it. When they said he could not have it, he felt like a child and they were the parent and this was as bad, if not worse, than feeling he was the immigrant and they society's gatekeepers.

But he would have it. He would. It was destiny. He could remember hardly anything from Torah study. And they do say no real memories are formed before age six; any you think you do have are false memories. But he was certain there was something he'd learned around five in a Torah portion, about a golden escalator. A moving staircase maybe, gilded by cherubim and seraphim just as the store had. So it was destiny and it would be his. Just not today. Not with this nose-to-lip ratio.

So, yes, by the afternoon, he felt vulnerable. And that's why he said, 'I'll collect her from school today.' And Melody turned to look at him, because, though he donated to whatever school Agata attended, he didn't ever show up there. Security had seen the diagrams of the campus and even had a replica model to practise a best exit for her in case of emergency. But the idea of him actually appearing there was a new and strange development.

CHAPTER 9

The girls went back to school the next day dizzy with the new information, their parents' buzz having kept them awake half the night like a dripping tap. Now, for the most part, they looked past the handsome carer, and made eye contact with Agata, who'd become, overnight, quite, quite visible to them.

Gail had, on the way to school, been distracted by the handsome Cypriot fruiterer, who, though a figure of fantasy, was not fiction. She'd paused to flirt over his wares, leaning coquettishly against a tray of starfruit as if they were headlights round her dressing-room mirror, had missed her bus and arrived at school late again. Her getting there ten minutes after the bell had gone was noted in a ledger. What wasn't noted was that she might have been on time, having bought an apple and heading for the bus stop, but the young fruiterer had said, 'Hey, come back! I want you to have this. This is a special lemon. An Iranian lemon. Completely different from an English lemon.'

She couldn't quite understand in what way he'd connected her to an Iranian lemon, so she focused on 'completely different'. A special lemon. Tart, and bright.

That's what it meant. The lemon meant he wanted to put a finger inside her as the boy had Faith. It was kind of a tacit agreement, and she weighed whether the finger, having touched so much citrus, might disrupt her vaginal pH. Maybe there were supplements she could start taking in advance to balance that.

Once in class, she was sent straight to her desk in the front row, and the French teacher's eyes were trained on her in such a way that meant she could not turn around to watch the now deeply visible Agata.

Now that she was more than just a girl in a wheelchair, she came more finely into focus, and the class saw she had long blonde hair and cat eyes. Her nose was upturned but broad, as if an illustrator's hand had got heavy and lazy in the middle of sketching Brigitte Bardot's face.

There had been no rumours about the new girl's arrival, such was the secrecy with which the family arrived at St Saviour's. If they'd known she was coming, the school would surely have prepped. As it was, the walls were shabby and the library books ageing. Given the state of the school, the fees must have seemed outrageous to the newcomers. Or perhaps they seemed a pittance to a man who had enough to buy one of the country's most iconic football clubs, enough to buy its most famous department store, if they had but let him.

By the time the bell went, she knew the arrival's name was Agata and that she had come from a mixed-sex school in West London.

She studied Agata from the side and later, during choir, at three-quarters. She could see that she was not Tribe. Her father, of course, was. ('They're trying to control the world with their money' tropes were often employed or at least hinted at by critics who suggested the purchase of the football club ought not to have gone through. And everyone knew he had been given an honorary Israeli passport.)

In each class, Agata fiddled with a pink fountain pen covered in Swarovski crystals. There were crystals, too, on her Mary-Janes, which sat on the wheelchair foot-rest, and with her flat, shiny hair and round, shiny blue eyes, she looked like something that required regular polishing. This school would be too dirty for her. The chewing gum repurposed for a new mouth after another girl had chewed it. The biro-scrawled band names on the sneakers of the sixth formers. Gail sensed she wouldn't be here long, feeling it as a premonition, like her interest in Natalie Wood's lifelong fear of drowning in dark water. What if you have no one with whom to share a premonition? No one to whom you can, as you drown, say 'I told you so!'

She looked for ways to approach Agata, but could not work past the other girls who had put themselves forward. Some pitched themselves as helpers. She was shocked to see Faith kneeling at her feet. And even more shocked when Agata made a motion with her hand indicating that her carer ought to wheel around her.

Finding herself alone at lunch time, she started a new letter to George, in which she outlined Agata's arrival.

She was so taken with her letter that it wasn't until the bell went and the girls who were suddenly so interested in their new fellow student rushed out and she looked up and saw that Agata was surrounded by no one, not even the man who wheeled her. *It must be a mistake*, she thought, and, tucking away the envelope, hurried to capitalise on it.

'Hi. We haven't been introduced yet,' she said, as if school were a cocktail party (come 8.30 for 9, dress code: business/casual), 'I'm Gail. Here. This is a Persian lemon.'

Gail couldn't tell if the girl had already noticed her as Agata delicately examined the fruit. With her bird-like physique, it looked like an aviary kingdom mating dance: she felt the weight in her slim hand. Smelled it. Held it against her cheek. She seemed to expect more from the citrus than it could offer, and suddenly dropped it into her lap, looking disappointed. Gail, who very rarely needed encouragement, was emboldened.

'It isn't like the English ones. It's not regular.'

'Uh huh.' She looked around for her carer. Faith was staring at them from across the room.

'You can keep it.'

'Are you OK?' asked Faith, materialising beside Agata. 'Is she bothering you?'

'No,' answered Agata, confused. As her carer returned, she nodded her head and said to Gail, 'Thank you.'

'You're welcome,' Gail replied, beaming. The carer wheeled her away, and Agata turned to look back at Gail who, once Faith was out of earshot, couldn't help but murmur under her breath, 'I'm going to help you.'

Agata was surprised to see her father waiting in the car for her, instead of just the chauffeur. He even stepped out to help her in, taking over from the carer.

'I've got this!' Ezra said, with an expression that hinted the carer should have *intuited* he wouldn't be needed for this task. Agata tried not to look at the place where his moustache and beard had been.

'How was your day?' he asked her.

'Is everything OK?' She looked at the gap between his nose and his lip, that vast, noisy flesh, the missing beard a metaphor for the guarded silence between them that she wished would return. It hadn't always been like this. Only since the wheelchair. Before he had always been too busy to talk with her about her day, but now, since the disease had progressed, he tried to find time for her – he just didn't know what to say. That was worse. Before this, she could at least make him say in her head what she needed him to say.

'Oh, absolutely fine. You don't have to worry about me. I don't ever want you worrying about me. Dad's got everything under control.'

She looked at him – she wanted to help hold together what she recognised was his fantasy of fatherhood, but she felt too weak to manage it. The expanse of skin between his nose and lip was mesmerising, and, to his despair, she had lost herself in it, silent. They were startled by a rap at the passenger window. The chauffeur snapped to attention, his bodyguard training ready to fight.

Agata sat upright.

'Oh,' she said, peering through the glass. 'That's a girl in my class.'

Ezra rolled down the window.

'Hello,' said Gail. 'Just saying hi and welcome to the school. I'm Gail,' she said to Ezra, 'I gave her a special lemon.'

Agata tapped her father's wrist and whispered, 'From Iran.'

'Why? Why from Iran?' snapped the driver and, sliding his hand through the partition, took it from them. Then he pressed a button to start closing the window, but Gail was not deterred.

'I just think that's what they call it,' said Gail, 'as a marketing thing. It's like an old lemon with a new name.'

'No,' said Ezra, 'we had this in the East End when I was young. It was a great delicacy for my family, it meant we had money that month.' And he took it back from the chauffeur/bodyguard and said thank you to Gail. Though sincere in his gratitude, he didn't offer her a lift and she thought it was because she wasn't pretty or interesting like Faith, not knowing it was because he was ashamed of his soft face.

'That was nice,' he said to his daughter as they drove away. 'That girl seems nice. Do you like her?'

Agata had to think about it. But her brain right now didn't allow for that. It was easy to be swept away. They heard the football crowds shrieking outside each pub they passed. She was so glad she wouldn't have to go to any more matches and interact with the footballers, who horrified her as they tried to express deference to her father, not sure what she – sexless but too old to be an adorable child – was meant to be. The sound of a goal and the yelling, so loud, so loud. He touched his soft lip in sadness as he watched her visibly wince at the raucous sound of public good cheer. 'Yes,' she said, so soft he had to lean in, 'I like her.'

CHAPTER 10

Within weeks of Agata's arrival it became known that Ezra Levy, having leftover cash from his inability to buy Parkers department store, was donating a large amount of money to build a new arts centre at St Saviour's. Maybe he added a dedicated arts wing whenever she arrived in a new school. Maybe it wasn't always art. Maybe sometimes science or history. There appeared to be no debate about whether or not to take his money, despite what the British papers knew but could not print.

'Hi!' Faith said, walking towards Agata, still trying to angle for her attention. She'd been placed in the dining hall and her carer had stepped back to allow her to chat uninhibited with the other girls. Faith was holding a lunch tray laden with meat and as she got closer, Agata's face wrinkled at the smell of it. Faith tried to make small talk: 'I like your pen you use in class.'

But either Agata could see that she hadn't actually particularly liked her pen, or she felt peculiar at Faith having noticed such a small detail, because she turned away. She was smiling tightly as she turned, as if Faith had asked her directions on the street in an unknown language. Faith might have recovered but instead made the error of briefly putting aside her lunch and excusing herself to the loo. They were young enough that pausing a conversation to go to the bathroom looked weak. Gail could hold in her urine for twenty-four hours if she had to and had been able to since the age of five. In an all-girls' secondary school, this was a more valuable talent than being able to hold your breath under water.

As they watched Faith retreat, Gail asked, 'Do you want me to push you somewhere?'

'OK. It's sunny.' Agata had a voice like new shoes she was trying to wear in. 'You can take me out to the courtyard.'

So Gail did, and the weight of the wheelchair against her body felt good, while the cool of the metal made her focus.

'You'd think your father would . . .'

'What?' Agata turned her head.

'I was just gonna say, you'd think your father would also donate money to make the school more wheelchair accessible. It wasn't enough just to alter the school entrance.'

'Oh, he'll get things changed.' She squinted in the sun. 'He always does.'

Then Gail took her gambit. 'I saw Faith came on strong with you.'

'That's not true. She only said she liked my pen . . .'

'She came on strong with me when I got here, too. It's hard to arrive at a school late. It's hard to see things clearly, like, all the things that are already in place, that you maybe don't know about.'

'What do you mean?'

Gail knew Faith would soon come looking for them and decided to switch approaches.

'Are you embarrassed getting picked up in a limousine?'

Agata said, 'No, why should I be?'

'Oh, just here, because all these rich girls think it's so uncool to have money.' She saw Agata's cheeks flush. 'Which is crazy, right, people pay a lot to be here. But you know, they punish the ones who make it visible. I'm glad that hasn't happened to you. You're brave. Not to be embarrassed.'

Agata stared at her, steely-eyed. *'We aren't the sort of people who talk about money.'*

'Come on.' Gail laughed. 'Tribe to tribe.'

'What do you mean?' Agata asked, her hands now on her wheels, ready to move away.

'The twelve tribes of Israel.' Gail shrugged, as if it were obvious. She didn't really know what she was talking about but she kept confidently riffing as she could see it having an effect on the girl.

Agata gripped the wheels. 'I don't know anything about that.'

'Would you like to? We have Jewish assembly here. It's just me and two other girls but . . .' Gail knew she sounded like a salesman, that her tone had taken on a sheen she'd not intended in her attempt to gain the upper hand.

Now Agata wheeled away from Gail as fast as she could.

'No, thank you. I'm English. That's all I am.'

Gail caught up with her in five big strides.

'OK. Well. You're also disabled so the Nazis would have got you on two counts.'

'I am not disabled.' She said it too loud. Girls swivelled their heads. Faith, having returned, stared, slack-jawed.

Gail bent down and said quietly, 'You're in a wheelchair. You can't walk.'

'I've only been in a wheelchair since I got here.' And she turned her head to address the room. '*Not that it's any of your business.*'

Gail couldn't concentrate in French as she tried to unpick this mystery. If you told her something was none of her business, she would crawl over broken glass to make it so. She could never concentrate in French, but it was usually about the cute Cypriot fruiterer or a movie or what she could say to help George Michael get back on the right track, or a resentment from when she was ten. Why? Why was Agata only recently in a wheelchair? What had happened to her?

Reaching no conclusion, at the lockers when the day was ending, she cracked and asked Faith:

'Why do you think Agata is in that wheelchair? Has she said anything to you?'

'Why?' sneered Faith, as she pulled on her lightweight coat. 'Are you going to try and *fix her*?'

'No,' Gail snapped, though she'd absolutely been intending to try to fix whatever was wrong.

Faith's voice was rigid: 'Maybe you should work on your own problems.' The impeccable posture of her words was undeniable.

'Maybe I should,' Gail mused, to try to show she wasn't hurt, her hurt framing each word in neon. 'Maybe I should try to work on my own problems.'

Then she tap danced it so everyone passing could watch, a toe-to-heel shuffle for each word: 'Maybe I should try to work on my own problems.'

Faith kept walking, and now Gail, following, spelled it out in sign language, which she'd learned when she'd volunteered at a summer camp for children with special needs: 'Maybe I should try to work on my own problems.'

Faith spun around.

'You're so weird and everyone hates you.'

It was said just as they left the school grounds, too late for Faith to notice that Dar was standing right there. Shocked, Dar pulled a gossamer turquoise scarf against her long neck as if to restrain herself.

Faith couldn't look at her and moved up the pavement as quickly as she could.

Dar knew she had to tread carefully given the recent blow-up over Faith. When the incendiary girl was out of earshot, Dar said to Gail: 'Everyone does not hate you.'

'I know.'

She wanted to slip her arm through Gail's but thought she'd better not risk it as there were still a lot of girls around.

'Maybe you *are* weird but I think that's a positive thing in this culture of sheep.'

'Mum. Why are you waiting for me?'

She noticed Gail said 'Mum' at the start, not end, of her accusation as a punctuation. Dar tried to be attuned to the rhythm of her daughter's speech as a literary critic might to a living-legend poet of advanced age. She parsed her lyrics like a Dylan-ologist. She never guessed correctly what the word placements meant, never guessed what it was she was *really* saying, since they meant nothing to Gail.

'I wandered over on the off-chance I'd make it in time. I got off work early, honey.' Gail was embarrassed to see her and to hear her say 'honey' – she felt herself covered in her mother's viscous, sticky presence and kept turning around to see what unpleasant thing might stick on her because of it. Her worst fear was that there might be a boy. A boy who'd want to make fun of her and would make more fun of her if she were with her mother. As if there were definitive proof that she was not born of air and sea, or definitive proof that she had by being born of human woman once touched a vagina and was therefore a lesbian and dirty with human frailty. As if her mother's screams as she'd emerged would call back through time and space and turn the boys' heads to stare at her.

This time, as she looked over her shoulder, she saw Agata being wheeled towards the limo. It seemed no one else was in it today. Only the carer.

'That's her,' Gail whispered.

'That's her?' said Dar, as bright as her turquoise scarf.

'Yeah.'

'Oh, God,' Dar sniffed, 'well, of course the daughter of Ezra Levy would be a chronic anorexic.'

Having removed her school tie with uncontestable fine motor skills, Agata padded, wobbly, towards the lift that went up to her bedroom. To get where she was going, she leaned on furniture pieces – the sofa to the coffee table to the credenza – like she had when she was a toddler. Standing in the doorway, Ezra saw this and it filled him with tenderness and sorrow. He himself needed to grip the sides of the banister to make it back upstairs, so struck was he by the image of her suffering.

His office door sealed, Ezra sank into his chair and put his hands on his marble desk, the cold of it lighting up the neural pathways to the recent past. How had he let this happen? What could he have done differently? What was he being punished for? He sat there in his office, calls on hold, flipping through the mental Rolodex. And, with the marble beneath his huge hands, he saw it clear as day: he had done nothing wrong. She was just very unwell.

In the family hierarchy, everyone relied on him and everything was his decision. Here is where Agata had tormented him. Her illness was out of his hands and then she'd taken it so far, it was out of her hands, too.

In the desolate period when her disease had first unfurled its flag, he found himself looking to his hands, to see if there was anything in them that might offer an answer, maybe a note written in the palm like when he had cheated on tests at primary school. They were big hands, and there was definitely nothing in them. He found, as the anorexia took hold, that he placed them on his wife's body more slowly, more mindfully, when they made love. She thought it was in wonder at her evermore refined body, but it was in wonder at his hands, his empty hands, which had no control over his daughter's body, having some control over his wife's body. Making love to her was always a relief as the battle waged on and on.

Agata had her own clear purpose to her sexuality. Because she could not understand how to get close to anyone, not to her father or her stepmother, or any girl at any school, she shaped her body into a sign declaring that she did not want to be touched. So she could tell herself it was an identity choice rather than a failure.

Other anorexics she encountered covered what they'd done with baggy clothing. But she went the other way, in belly tops and shortened skirts. She'd never tried to hide what she'd become. She'd let everybody see it. And she'd chewed and chewed gum every waking hour to stave off hunger pangs. 'Stop that,' Ezra would say. 'Why?' 'It's not classy,' he replied. And she laughed, because his East End accent was still so strong after all these years.

Sitting at his desk, trying to pinpoint Day Zero, he remembered, suddenly, stupidly, Agata's ill-fitting brides-maid dress at their wedding. That it had, apparently, been the right size at the fitting a month earlier. But come the day it gaped on her. He hadn't noticed, he supposed because he'd been too busy getting married. And his new wife had looked so lovely and so slim – yes, slimmer than other 'regular' women. But that wasn't her fault, she was from an Eastern Bloc country and had grown up with poor nutrition. It wasn't like she'd tried to be thin (he told himself).

Agata appeared at his door and, rising from his desk – 'Are you tired, honey?' – he wrapped his arm around her and her sharp shoulder blades pressed into him. He felt fleshy and stupid and like the two truths fed each other. He thought of his mother who had a special chair that Cousin Jacob wasn't allowed to sit in because, she explained to Jacob, he was fat and would break it. Agata was supposed to be his own build, genetically. Not fat, just solid. But what is solid when it's transferred from a father and placed onto a daughter? And he supposed that she had simply worked very hard, with foresight and dedication and what he now took to be a spiritual will, not to be anything like him.

*

Dar's long history as a protestor whose causes existed to her in black and white was occasionally useful, her unflinching directness of vision making Gail's life simpler in certain respects. She wondered how she could not have seen what Dar had instantly recognised as a serious eating disorder. She attributed her oversight to every girl at school being touched with anorexia to some degree or other. Even Lilah, the one overweight girl, said she was suffering from an eating disorder. But no one had taken it as far as Agata. Perhaps it wasn't that she had greater willpower than the others. Maybe she was simply the one with the means to end up being wheeled between classes.

Dar was still talking about it at dinner (here, once she had made her point but kept going, was where she became un-useful to Gail, again).

'The amount of poison he's injected into British society, of course that poison has seeped into his own blood.'

'That sounds . . .'

'What?' said Dar as she pushed the peas onto her fork.

'It sounds kind of antisemitic.'

'It just so happens it's correct in this particular case. The filth he has on that TV channel. The filth he allows on the front page of his newspaper. He is an awful blood-sucking parasite poisoning the well of British culture.'

As she vented, she was kind of talking about him, mainly. But there was a secret part of Dar that felt mistreated by her daughter and was talking about her. Maybe everyone encouraged to rail against a popular figure by a tabloid newspaper or programme is really talking about the family member they love the most but can't find a way to get close to.

CHAPTER *11*

Dar had an abrupt turnaround the next day, when girls were handed invitations that read 'Agata Levy is having a sixteenth birthday party'. Gail had looked around her, expectant, before the hope slowly faded from her face. She'd then covered as fast as she could that she'd ever been expecting an invite, as if she had not actually wanted to be asked. Then a whole new expression passed over her face when she saw the look of pain on Lilah's. Faith, holding an invitation, smirked over at her.

Throughout the day, Gail stayed far away from both Agata and Faith and made sure not to be ambushed for any possible allegiance with Lilah. When she thought everyone was distracted and she could get away with it, she'd slice off and consume little slivers of anxiety as to why this had happened to her when she'd worked so hard.

That evening, Dar was staring deep, deep into the fridge, like Elizabeth Taylor examining a man's soul when, without tearing her eyes from a wilted tuna sandwich, she remembered to ask, 'How was school?' Gail must have been too tired to hold the cards close to her chest as, having meant to keep it back, she quickly told Dar everything.

'Agata is having a sixteenth birthday party and she hasn't invited me.'

'Who?'

'The Levy daughter. She handed out the invitations in class this morning.'

Dar slammed the fridge door shut and turned slowly.

'Did they invite Faith?'

Gail could face seeing Faith in the corridors but her name still made her flinch. She didn't like where Dar was going with this, could sense a cause coming on, like shivers the day before a flu.

'Yes. Everyone is invited except me and Lilah.' Gail measured Dar's facial reaction with each new revelation like she was an hour by hour weather forecast.

'Fat Lilah?'

'I wouldn't phrase it that way. I think she's just voluptuous.'

'Call it what it is, just like we know *exactly* why they haven't invited YOU.'

Gail nodded, even though she didn't exactly know why, only that it could have been many things about her. That they were not wealthy. That between her making inroads with Agata and the invitations being handed out, Faith had spread rumours about her. Maybe Agata had even wanted to invite her, but her father's security had done due diligence on all the girls' families and been alerted to Dar's left-wing activism. But she knew what her mother was driving at.

'Why would us being Jewish be a problem for them if they're Jewish, too?'

'Because it draws attention to it at a time when he's toadying up to the establishment harder than ever before.

He's still smarting from them spanking his arse with the department store.'

Gail flinched at this monstrous image.

'I really don't see how one Jewish teen at his Jewish teenager's birthday party could tip the balance for him. How would the establishment even know I'd been there?'

Dar leaned her back against the fridge as if for strength. 'You don't understand how they work.'

'Who is "they"?'

'It. You don't understand how *it* works.'

'Oh,' answered Gail, leaning her weight from one socked foot to another, 'is IT an upgrade from THEY?'

'Yep. They're all interlinked. The headmistress is just the smallest doll inside a matryoskha set, of which the House of Lords is the largest.'

There were a lot of buildings being erected in Dar's suspicious imagery. Gail wished she knew parkour so she might scramble to make better sense.

In the morning, Dar sprang into action, silently unhooking a skirt suit from the closet, where it hung behind her many pairs of corduroy trousers. With no appointment booked, she went to the headmistress four weeks after they'd last been summoned there. She marched just the way she had marched when she took infant Gail in her buggy on a nuclear disarmament protest (when her wedge heels slowed her and they ended up very, very far back in the march, alongside what was then called Dwarves for Peace).

As Dar waited to be admitted, Gail prodded her.

'Mum.'

'Yeah?'

'What if there's no issue except Agata doesn't like me?' she whispered. She didn't want it to be true, but, unlike her mum, she accepted it was a possibility. 'What if there's nothing nefarious, you're just crazy?'

Dar refused to whisper. 'Don't say that.'

'It is a possibility, isn't it?'

Her mother straightened her spine. 'I'm just mad as hell, and I'm not going to take it any more.'

'Yeah, but, Mum, just quoting a movie doesn't mean you're right.'

'You wanted to go to this party, yes?'

Gail answered, warily, 'I don't know if I wanted to go. I was expecting to be invited.'

Dar puffed up with the helium of a cause, which allowed her to feel free but also to look down on people. It was a kind of self-soothing after a difficult day at work or a morning balancing bills. 'Then I'm getting you invited.'

'Do I have to be here?'

Her mother turned to her but didn't reply.

'So it was a paper invitation? Not an email?'

'No, Mum, it was . . . it looked like it was actually embossed on some kind of metal.'

This fired her up more. 'What kind of metal?'

'What difference does it make?'

'I want the facts correct before I go in there. Metal! Ridiculous!'

The door opened. The second time they'd been there in one month, this was not at all the norm. As disappointed as the headmistress had been in Gail over the Parliament Hill fantasy fellatio, at least the essay had provided a jolt of shock and excitement. Now she looked exhausted to see them.

The truth was, wrestling with middle age, the headmistress didn't want to spend her time with a woman even older than her, someone whose life decisions had aged her and who was now bringing trouble to her doorstep.

'I don't think Gail needs to be here,' said the headmistress, not hiding the audible sigh. 'She should be running along to . . .'

'To French,' offered Gail, wanting very much not to be involved. It was always French she seemed to be due at, always, even though she had absorbed no French. She felt an echo of this every time she waited at the dentist, thumbing a magazine she did not subscribe to but had always somehow read.

Dar couldn't say out loud that she wanted her daughter to watch her advocate for her, against what she'd explained was the establishment, so she'd be impressed and maybe treat her better.

She smoothed her skirt, ready to give a performance that would reverberate around the whole school. Kids would be talking about it so much it would boost Gail's popularity, as her father's cinema had boosted hers. She had it in her head that the number-one thing teenagers today go wild for is the forced implementation of fairness.

She could not explain to her daughter or herself, and certainly not the headmistress, why she had elected to insert her child inside an establishment she had also made various appointments to rail against. As she cleared her throat, the position was weak and they both knew it.

The headmistress would have had all the power, but Dar's scent threw her off, unbalanced her a little. Foreign.

So foreign! Good foreign or bad foreign? A Silk Road smell. She didn't know it was saffron.

Dar settled in her seat. The headmistress picked up the scent again, tried to sit back and smile and disguise her affrontment. They shouldn't have been back here until the school had made their decision on Gail's place. They shouldn't have been back here until judgement day. And so her own performance was diluted.

'It isn't right,' Dar said, 'this business with the Levy birthday invites getting handed out. Embossed on metal, I heard! You cannot allow this. A child should invite the whole class, or they should invite none of them.'

Without a response, Dar was already negotiating. 'My child shouldn't have to watch the invites being handed out.'

Through the window Dar could see the students, could see Gail hobbling in her long skirt. They couldn't rightly be called children.

'They aren't children though, are they?' the headmistress quibbled.

Dar sat up straight. 'But they're also not adults. What else are you going to let them choose for themselves? I thought this school prided itself on strict rule-keeping.'

'No,' the headmistress looked confused, 'not really. Why did you think that?'

'Well, I thought that because of the detailed uniform requirements.'

'No, that's just for show.'

'Gail says having to always wear the blazer with the school insignia just helps other schools identify you if they want to shout, "Oi, Bitch!"' Dar shouted it: 'Like, "Oi, Bitch!" Like that.'

'I don't think that happens very often.'

'Let's stay on topic,' said Dar, and the headmistress did hate her and in her head, she did say, 'This NHS nurse. This immigrant Jew.' And then she backpeddled from both and, in case there was a camera that could see into her mind, having been a bit racist and classist, immediately gave in to her demands.

By the time Dar left, Agata had been forced to add Gail and Lilah to her guest list. Dar left, wobbly with achievement as if success were a pair of stilettos sawn at one heel. On the top deck of the bus that afternoon, it dawned on Gail that her mother could live happily with any societal wrong, so long as she could first be allowed to march in protest against it.

CHAPTER 12

The day of the party, though Dar had criticised Ezra Levy and, more pointedly, the school for allowing such a criminal to enroll their child, Gail could tell she was excited. She had Gail try on some of her clothes. They were doing mother–daughter things they'd not done forever, like in a touching movie. Dar pulled out face masks and chilled tea bags for their eyes and they lay on the sofa listening to George Michael sing 'Jesus to a Child', which wasn't their religion, but was still very soothing, the way the conviction of other people's beliefs can be.

But, as much as she wanted to stay in this mother–daughter cocoon, Dar broke the spell.

'You know how Ezra Levy made his first million? Before the newspapers and TV and fast fashion? Copper money,' she said from under her tea bags. 'Copper. You know what that means?'

Gail scratched her stomach. 'That he made his fortune in copper?'

'That he's a *murderer*. That there was no opposition to stem his move up the hierarchy because the opposition was offed. Ashkenazi Jews – they're not like us.'

'Why not?'

'They can't tolerate alcohol.'

'Neither can English people. It seems a weird reason to take against a whole people.'

'They're *not like us.*'

She peeled off her face mask.

'They think they're better than us because they "invented" socialism.'

'Well, if they invented socialism, why would they think they're better than us . . .'

'They think they're better because we're from the desert.'

'We're *all* originally from the desert. Right?'

'Yes, yes, sure.' In her verve, Dar was squeezing the tea bags that had been on her eyes until they began to burst their seams. 'But all their desert traces have washed out in the laundry. He doesn't know anything about people like us. He doesn't know we exist, brown and broke.' She didn't say 'poor'. She didn't say 'working class'. 'Broke', always 'broke'.

As if they were still beneficiaries of the wealth her dad had had in Iraq, before the government took it from him on the way out of the country. Because broke implies for now and that it's all going to swing back. But how long do you wait for the return before you move on and accept this is who you are now?

Gail fixed on the first part of the sentence, scoffing, 'Mum. We aren't that brown. You aren't. We just tan easily. To be honest, Mum, he's probably darker than you. And he does know I exist. I gave him a lemon.'

'Was he grateful?' she shrieked. This was why they never let her have the megaphone on a march. The shriek magnified through tin could only lose hearts. 'Did he even say thank you? See!'

'He was grateful, actually.'

Dar raised her eyebrows like a private eye in a forties noir. 'Why didn't you *tell me this*?'

'Oh, God, what does it matter?'

'He's not good for the Jews, and he isn't good for us! He makes all of us look bad. All that conspicuous consumption in an era of austerity. The sweatshop fast fashion and the disgusting sexualised ads for it I've been shielding you from since you were eleven. He makes our lives harder.'

'I read his wife has a couture line now.'

'Oh, God, who could possibly care?'

'Then why am I going? You forced this to happen!'

'I did the right thing.' She sighed and changed tack. 'We need to keep tabs on him. I'm glad you're going.'

But she was glad for a different reason that she could never let on, one that made her more and more excited.

Dressed and made-up, they drove down past the strange energy of Spaniard's Inn, then through the concrete overpasses of Swiss Cottage and finally on to the splendour of St John's Wood. They passed women with luxury bags and colourful headscarves, whom Dar studied in the rear-view mirror.

'What, Mum?'

'Just guessing if those beautiful women are Syrian or Palestinian.' She squinted. 'Probably Syrian.'

'I'm sorry, are you an ethnographic researcher now?'

'I could be. I'd probably be good at it.'

After they found the broad road with the visible security guard both on the pavement and outside the mansion itself, Dar parked the Camry a little way up.

Dar squeezed her hand. 'What are you going to do if you see him?'

'Oh, Mum!' Gail sighed. She felt like George Michael batting away a silly chat-show query about his drug use, and made her mum leave her there.

'Hey,' said Dar, in her most beseeching voice, 'will you do me a favour? Will you come by the hospital after so everyone can see how amazing you look?'

Gail told her she thought that was crazy but then she looked into her mum's face and it was so soft. She suddenly saw how badly Dar wanted to be there herself. That maybe Dar went to the rallies because there were no gala invites. Everyone is invited to a protest. Gail wondered how much she might have wanted to go to the NHS thank-you concert, when George Michael gave the tickets to the nurses. She felt, then and there, that Dar hadn't had a ticket as she had claimed, only perhaps that she had wanted one, and had made the rest up. Gail understood. It's not a crime to make up things that feel like they should be true.

She said she'd see how she went and then she let her mother hug her.

'Be careful, please,' Dar whispered in her ear, despite having instigated a protest to ensure Gail's invitation.

If Gail had allowed her mother to trail her, the first thing she'd have noticed was that Ezra Levy's house was gigantic but contained very little, like a large porcelain plate holding a tiny, curated meal. What *was* there looked to have been purchased on the fly. Nothing handed down, no prized-for-generations Ottoman kilims.

There *was* a Kandinsky and Gail stood before it for a long time while classmates passed her on their way downstairs. Gail was much more dressed up than the intended invitees, who were in low-slung jeans and belly tops, girls who exemplified their mothers' belief that there is no good fashion beyond the 'Freedom '90' video.

'Where's Agata?' she asked them, balancing a gift in her hand – the collected works of Isaac Bashevis Singer. There was an array, on a credenza, of gifts wrapped and accented with sparkles, pom poms and ribbons. She could tell there were no books, as she added hers to the pile.

In the basement was an Olympic-length swimming pool, but, though she felt fine about her body in a bathing suit, Gail could only do a kind of puppy paddle that made people think she needed saving when she didn't. A woman she took to be Agata's mother (then understood to be her stepmother, Melody) was already in the pool. Dressed in a high-necked swimsuit, her skin was porcelain and high-gloss, like a vanity sink that gets daily housekeeping.

She was still a young woman but, after multiple minor tweaks over the years, her face was like an unplaceable accent. Her husband knew her face had changed since he'd first met her, but even if he'd studied all the paparazzi and opening-night photos, he couldn't exactly place how.

The teenage girls, spray tanned, got in around her like serfs, dirty from the day. It was meant to be Agata's celebration, but, having handed her their gifts, the girls' attention quickly moved towards Melody. How could it not? She had a flattering question for each of them, which she swam right up close to ask. It was flirting adjacent.

Ezra had not had to flirt with his wife to woo her, not really. Rather, he had made her an offer and she had accepted and it had worked out well for both of them. She was beautiful and stylish, with a mostly warm heart. Everything was above board, and he of all people knew the difference.

She found out, after their second date, that Ezra was big. At the start, after sex, she would cup his penis until he, like it, was fast asleep. It was hers. He was hers. After the divorce from his first wife, others of approximately Melody's ilk had failed to plant their flag in him. She, from her oft conquered nation, knew how to and she held on to his penis like a flag. The sex had always been great. She found him overpowering in the best way. He liked saying her name with his surname pressed against it. He very quickly loved her.

She lay on her back in the water, looking at the ceiling, which they'd modelled on a Turkish hammam, shooting the plaster through with cut-out stars that, in sunlight or a bright moon, were projected onto the body of the swimmer below. The row of diamond stars she wore in her ears glittered back at the sun shards, separated lovers reaching towards each other.

As Melody floated there, the centre of a Busby Berkeley movie, Lilah, sitting on a plastic chaise in the corner, looked miserable to be wearing a swimsuit. Dar's social victories never really took into account whether the oppressed group wanted the particular freedom she was intent on securing for them.

Agata, standing with her feet on the bottom of the pool, holding the marble side so you couldn't see her body, looked neither pleased nor displeased to see Gail, simply saying: 'You're here.'

Gail agreed that she was and started to back away. A few girls floated around the birthday girl – Faith swam back and forth between the child and her mother, unsure of who could better advance her needs, because she still didn't know what her needs were.

Then a sound came echoing around the marble and Gail knew in her gut that this signalled Ezra's arrival. His footsteps were loud, and she heard him before she saw him, the first time she'd seen him standing up. Usually, in London, you get to see people standing all the time, on the Tube, at bus stops, and if you like what you see you can initiate conversation. The exception is if they're very rich and then there's less opportunity to view their bodies as wholes. That's why the rich often have to just marry each other.

Ezra made a great show of helping his wife from the pool and drying her off, separating her toes as she tried to shoo him away. The girls were giggling, fascinated. He threw an inflatable flamingo towards his daughter in the water – the item was ridiculous, both in his hands and when it left them, in the air, but it made sense once it hit the pool. This was for show – Agata was far too delicate to throw things at. He'd never have dared if strangers weren't watching.

Gail whispered to Lilah: 'How better to crown an underground lap pool that has enraged and flooded neighbours but with a flamingo that will take a hundred years to degrade?'

'Please don't talk to me,' said Lilah.

Ezra removed a shoe and splashed the water with his bare foot. When the water splashed back against his trouser leg, he frowned as if a stranger in a pub had knocked his pint. In his one shoe, he left, immediately, stonily brushing it off his suit. What did he think would happen if you splash water? It was some steps beyond no longer remembering the price of a pint of milk.

Agata stayed where she was, still holding the side, now floating her legs out behind her. In the water she was free. Her body wasn't strained or sore. She floated not like a queen, not like she was on display the way Melody was, more like a lily pad, as if she had roots and calm and purpose. She didn't want to get out even though the other girls were beginning to shiver and prune.

Gail was slightly hypnotised by the dancing light from Melody's earrings. Then she came back into her body and wandered upstairs. Passing the kitchen, she saw they were prepping snacks on long counters, a chef bent over, moving sushi like chess pieces.

All the visible staff were too occupied to notice her. The idea came to her as if written on the palm of her hand in an exam: why not just keep exploring the house? At first, Gail ascended the staircase cautiously, afraid of being stopped. Once she'd made it to the first floor, it was easy to just keep going. The staircase seemed to have a story embedded in its ironwork – Persephone and Demeter of Greek myth? – but she didn't slow down to figure it out.

On the third floor, she could smell him, the animal smell excreted not only from sex or violence but from planning a next move. She followed it like Pepé Le Pew, this being the problem in what was to exist between them: he was a real animal and she was a cartoon rendering of an animal. The door was closed but she knew it was him behind it. She knocked and turned the doorknob without waiting for a reply. He was sitting at his desk, in an office where the books had clearly been colour-coded by a designer. Gail wondered if the designer had been a man or a woman and if their hand had shaken from being in his home as they placed them there.

His stubble having grown in, he was better looking than when she'd seen him in the limo. He looked like a bear you would hold onto in your childhood bed crossed with a bear that could kill you. His hair was luxuriant but out of step, a George Michael look a decade old, something George would look back on and good-naturedly mock.

'What are you doing up here?' Ezra's voice was as flat as a wheat field, none of the cockney cheeriness from the lemon handover in the car. The ambience was quite different in his own smallish quarters of his own giant home from that in his moving vehicle, like he needed the containment of speed or his bonhomie exploded.

'What are any of us doing here? It's like Dostoevsky said' (she felt mad, crazed with ambition alone in his presence, knowing her mother would be out of her mind with curiosity and, yes, *jealousy* at what she'd done), "The mystery of human existence lies not in just staying alive, but in finding something to live for."'

He stared at her like he might leap across the table. Then he laughed, angry, impatient and maybe trying for charm, but it was beyond his bear-paw grasp. His laugh trailed off like old soul songs that lower the volume at the end instead of actually finishing.

'I know you. You gave me a lemon.'

'I really did,' she replied. Flirting, as best she could grasp, could be fashioned from scrambled syntax. Scramble the expected rhythm of a sentence so a big, strong, famous man was thrown off his guard.

'Was your sushi chef flown here from Japan?'

'From Istanbul,' he answered, eyes on the papers in front of him.

'I've always wanted to go there. You go there a lot . . . for business?'

For a moment, she thought he was looking at her chest but then understood he was glancing at her Star of David pendant. It seemed to seal a deal for him. He hated her for her nose, the texture and colour of her hair. She repulsed him. Their conversation was over.

'You're lost,' he said.

'I know where I am.' Growing up with the smartphone function to 'unsend' texts had made teenage girls bold in ways that couldn't be taken back.

'The birthday party is down in the pool.'

But she wouldn't go away.

'What are you working on?'

He sighed, looking around the room for a security guard and finding only a penguin paperweight.

'I'm . . . working on work.'

'That's what I say when my mum tries to check my homework.'

Then suddenly:

'Are you going to try again to buy Parkers?'

He looked up but not at her, his eyes clouded with something that looked painful and she only realised later was pain.

'I hope so.'

'You haven't given up?' When she said 'up' her voice

went up and he noticed it and also noticed she was short
for her age.

'Nope,' he said curtly and pressed a button on his desk.

'My mum says you're only trying to buy it to be part of
the British establishment. She's an NHS nurse.'

He pushed himself up to his full height. 'Well, I
certainly wish your mother the best of luck inside her
crumbling system. Can you fuck off?'

'What?'

'I said, and I don't like to repeat myself, you're in the
wrong place. The party is downstairs.'

He physically guided her out, but as he got to the far
end of the room, he paused and reached into a bookshelf,
reaching across her, his thick arm brushing her breast.

'This is a first edition.'

He handed her a Dostoevsky collection, heavy and unread.

'For you to keep. But first you have to leave.'

She clasped it to her chest. 'After I've finished it, I'll
give it back.'

'It's OK. It's nothing. Now will you go?'

'Have you ever read it?'

He looked as bewildered as a man learning a new
language with a different alphabet.

'No. It was put there. Everything was.'

She noticed it then, on the shelf.

'Is that my lemon?'

'Fuck's sake. I suppose it is.'

She walked over and touched it. She made a point of
touching it without asking, feeling his irritation so intense
it floated from his body and up towards the ceiling.

'Can you . . .' he drifted off.

'Well, if you're not going to use that lemon, I'll take it back. It was given to me by a man with a crush on me.'

She waited for him to click that she'd said 'man' and not 'boy'.

'No, I'll keep it.' He took it back from her and returned it to the shelf. 'I am using it.'

'How?'

'I look at it.'

'That's it?'

He exhaled, visibly deflating.

'It makes me think. So that's nice.'

'You could taste it and it might make you think even more things.' She stared at him. 'Oh. You got given them when your family was having a good month. You don't want to remember too much about your childhood in the East End, maybe.'

'Maybe. How old are you?'

He asked because she held and maintained eye contact in a manner he'd never encountered in a teen.

'I'm in your daughter's class. So I'm the same age as your daughter,' adding, 'my mum fucking hates you.' She enjoyed him asking her age and enjoyed the follow-up of saying 'fuck' to him.

'Yeah, you made your point.'

He went back to his desk and his laptop, not looking up.

'Are you not coming back down to the birthday?'

'I've already shown myself. That's me done for the day.'

She stepped closer and he covered his work with his hand and she saw that part of him was still a school child.

'It was nice to chat. Good day.'

She turned at the doorway.

'Do you find it hard to look at her?'

He didn't answer. She continued.

'The first day, the first day I saw her at school, I found it really hard. Just seeing her like that. It was a proper jump scare. I can't imagine it's something you get used to. Especially as a dad.'

She lowered her voice an octave and it ran through his body when she said:

'I know you're doing your best.'

He held back tears. He might have let one escape down his cheek, but security knocked on the door, entering without waiting for a response.

'You OK in there?'

'We're OK, she got lost. Say hello to your mother from me.'

The girls were out of the pool and gathered around the low dining table of the den when she wandered back in.

'Where is she?'

Faith shrugged. Lilah, now dressed, holding her arms around herself as if still in her bathing suit, whispered to her and Gail nodded. Lilah pointed up the hall.

'Well, don't just go wherever you like,' snapped Faith. Gail turned on her heel and, as if channelling the look Ezra had given in the office, stared at Faith until she shrank back. She shrank even though she had been invited to the party in the first place when Gail had not.

Then Gail went up the hall, doing what she liked, until she came to another closed door. But this one, unlike Ezra's, was not sealed but left slightly ajar. Enough that she could stand back and peer through.

Agata was being dried, since she was too weak after the swim to dry herself. She hadn't the energy after any swim for the last few months, and the therapists had made drying herself a goal she was working up to. It was challenging for whoever was helping her – if you went too rough, her skin could tear like a rice-paper page from the makeup blotters the girls tucked into their school pencil cases. Her dad had tried at Christmas, in St Barts, after she'd been peacefully floating in the crystal ocean. She looked so happy and free, everything seemed possible: that she could recover, that money was worth fighting for because it meant you could buy peace. Once the damage was done by his huge hands, neither could speak to the other for the rest of the trip. He had tried and succeeded in hurting people with his hands before. But he had forgotten, when it happened with the towel, that he had ever caused anyone physical harm in his past and had looked, in amazement and bewilderment, where he'd harmed her. He stood there, frozen, until he saw the tears streaming down her face.

Gail kept watching, the volume of her breathing turned as low as she could go. When she had finished with Agata, Melody stepped out of her own wet swimsuit and into a waiting outfit that was hung from a satin hanger on a hook. Her body looked like a country that had never been invaded. It had been colonised only with the finest, most lightweight polymer implants, scarless, imperceptible, as delicate as her own silk threaded through fabric, invisibly holding the design together. Looking up at her stepmother, Agata seemed almost to crack open, the light turned up brighter in her blue eyes beneath the stretched-taut face.

For a moment Melody had the sweater on over her head; she was no face and just breasts, and, still watching, Gail felt like a man must feel seeing such a thing, the blotting out of the woman's individual personality so she was just a page in an old *Playboy* that could only fit bits of a female on each page, no choice but to split them into parts. All the party invitees had bodies that were still in flux. Agata's efforts were proof that you could pull it into reverse. Melody's efforts allowed her to construct herself a whole other way.

A light was turned on in the hall and Gail went from shadow to a suddenly illuminated figure. She saw that Agata could make her out. And they recognised in each other's eyes the fire. And now they had a secret. Though they couldn't quite name it, they both had something over the other, never mind that it was the same thing. It didn't yet occur to them that one of them might, with their secret shared fire, rush to put the embers out while the other bent to stoke them.

Gail called her mother to tell her the party would go on a lot longer and then went to leave early. On her way out she removed a series of sparkly pom poms from other people's gifts and attached them to the Isaac Bashevis Singer book.

'Caught you!' said a voice she didn't know, apart from having heard this timbre a million times from a million boys as she walked through the park.

She turned around slowly.

'What are you doing?'

She squinted. It was a man of maybe twenty-five or twenty-six, who had a pretty enough face ruined by his hair. He was wearing what looked like a beret, only it was made out of his hair, it was a *haircut*. It was, in its origins, intended to mimic Afro-Caribbean hair but he was extremely white, with an Irish accent. He was wearing an expensive casual outfit where the top and bottom matched each other but neither matched him.

'I'm Gail.'

'Like the coffee shops? Haha. If I take you for one is it on you?' He spoke 'Haha' as a word rather than laughing in action.

'No. Because I'm sixteen.'

'So . . . you can date?'

'I really focus on . . .' she figured out what she focused on. 'On my studies.'

'OK, OK, respect.' When he said 'respect' he made what she took to be a mark of respect with his hands, like someone would mime the 'check, please' motion across a room to a waiter. She looked around because she didn't want to be seen with him but saw, to her confusion, that there were girls staring at her who looked like they wanted to talk to him.

'And you are?'

He cleared his throat. 'What do you mean?'

'What's your name?'

He started to laugh, real not 'Haha', and put his hand on his stomach, a move that seemed the cousin of his 'respect' mime.

She squinted as she tried to parse the expressions of the watching girls. He wasn't in any boy band that she could remember. 'Are you on Ezra's football team?'

'Why don't you know who I am? I scored the penalty

that won the last two games.'

'So why are you here at a birthday party for a sixteen-year-old?'

'You know,' he leaned in conspiratorially, nodding at the girls behind them, 'you know how girls are about footballers.'

She pretended not to see them nor understand him. 'No.'

Furrowing his brow, he ignored her. She was shocked to see that though he was young, his brow would not line when he attempted expression. Talking it through with Dar later when she gave her the edited breakdown of the day's events, she understood he was already using Botox.

'Ezra's been so good to me, I try to be good to his fam.'

'What does fam mean?'

He started to back down, clearly wishing he wasn't being watched by a throng, and whispered, 'It's short for "family".'

'Right,' and she leaned in and whispered, 'I don't think Agata particularly wants you here. Do you see her anywhere? I mean, I don't think she cares one way or another.'

'That's hard to say, she's not been well . . .'

Now she was competitive.

'Are you going to help her?'

He stepped back, raking a nervous hand through his hair-hat.

'I just try and support the family the way they've supported me.'

Melody floated by and the young man was instantly reinvigorated, twinkling at her. When she leaned in and kissed his cheek, the blood flushed to his face and maybe elsewhere. Then she floated away. The young man was doggedly earthed. It was hard to imagine him airborne enough to ever score a goal let alone be their best player.

She studied him to check she understood what she was looking at. He was definitely a young man, kind of a man, an in-between creature like a man with the back half of a horse but with Botox – it dawned on her as he talked that he was half-man and half-footballer.

'I come from a really tight-knit family,' he continued, when there was no encouragement for an encore.

I don't care, she thought, *I'm not interested*, and there was a brief pause while she tried to ascertain if she'd said that out loud. She knew she must not have because he pleasantly asked:

'Are you going to swim?'

'I have already,' she lied, the girls turning to each other with wide eyes. 'I've got to go.'

'See you around?'

Not answering, she left, smiling to herself, walking briskly. As she exited the home, she high-fived a security guard who wouldn't respond and this made her laugh out loud. 'HAHA' she burst out, and clasped her stomach as the footballer had, which only made her more hysterical.

PART 3

CHAPTER *13*

On Monday, she used the Dostoevsky book as a pillow, lying at the end of the hockey field, while Faith huddled with the other girls, their good looks underscored by their powerful athleticism. Summer had been on its way in only to be met, at the door, by a three-day cold snap, bright but chilly. The girls were brimming with rage as they bashed the puck with their sticks. Gail pictured a hapless passerby pounded by football hooligans. She took a brief rest while the girls she considered foolish played, opening her eyes to a bright blue sky.

Agata was in her wheelchair at the other end of the pitch, her carer at a discreet distance. Gail wondered, now, if he was also her bodyguard, for when the puck came too close, he picked it up and handed it back with what she determined to be a cold anger. But he might have actually just been cold. Agata had a blanket around her.

Gail stood up, stretched, and walked along the side and up to them. She nodded at the carer and he stepped aside.

'Why are they making you watch this?'

Agata shielded her eyes, maybe from the sun, maybe from Gail. 'I want to watch it.'

Gail couldn't imagine that it was pleasant for her to watch a whole team of strong and healthy bodies in motion while she sat, withered, on the side.

'Did you enjoy your party?'

'Of course.' Agata paused, still reintegrating into conversation as a skill after so long in hospital. 'Did you?'

'I thought it was a lovely event. My mother can be difficult and embarrassing. Sometimes I want to kill her.'

At this, Agata could not help but be interested.

'But I also still like sleeping in her bed on a Sunday with the newspaper,' added Gail, 'reading the style section while she reads the political analysis.'

'That sounds nice.' Agata's own voice felt odd in her throat, like maybe she should spit it out. 'Why are you telling me?'

Gail laid it on the table: 'Because she made you invite me to your party.'

Agata, as was her nervous tic, placed her hands on either side of her wheelchair as if ready to race. 'That's not true, you were always invited.'

'Oh, really?'

'Yes, I think the metal of the invites stuck together and Faith got two instead of one. She must have just ended up with yours.'

'Oh. That's it?' Gail stepped back, removing herself from a line-up. So she wasn't a criminal interloper after all. She ought to have been relieved, but as soon as the role was rescinded, she kind of missed it. 'That's all that happened?'

'Yes. It was only Lilah who wasn't meant to be invited.'

'Because she's fat?'

'I don't think she's fat. And that's not very nice to say.'

Gail bent down so her face was at the same level as Agata's as she answered:

'. . . said the girl who had declined to invite her? Isn't that less nice?'

Agata, recognising this tone of dominant tenderness from her father, moved her fingers from the sides of her chair to the spokes of its wheels. She was instinctively searching for something to hurt herself with and catching herself in time, hissed:

'Lilah's uncle in the House of Lords blocked my father's purchase of the department store.'

'Oh, wow. Really?' She liked how genuinely angry Agata looked. She liked that she could finally make out emotion in her flattened features.

'Yup. My dad's still smarting. He's the one who tried to stop her coming.'

'Until my mum ruined it.'

'Yeah.'

Gail now knelt on the grass so she was lower than Agata.

'It's kind of a trashy store, don't you think?'

Agata smiled and made direct eye contact, an invisible ruler recording the space between their faces. 'I do! That's what I told my dad! The gilded fucking escalator!'

'The cherubim and seraphim!'

They both pretended to vomit, a gesture Agata knew more intimately than most. When they were done, they wiped their mouths of invisible puke and smiled at each other.

'It would be fun,' mused Gail, 'to break in there one day and get high and look at the gilded cherubim and seraphim on the ceiling.'

Agata wheeled a little closer so there was barely an inch between them.

'Is that the kind of thing you do?'

'I haven't before,' said Gail, 'but I would for you.'

Agata blushed. She knew this tone; she knew it so well.

'Your stepmother doesn't seem like a bad person. Not like a stepmother in a story.'

Agata snorted. 'She's a kindly idiot.'

Ah, but they both knew Gail had spied on the ease between them.

'She's beautiful.'

'What an achievement.' Agata's sarcasm was magnified by the metal in which she was enthroned.

'Well,' said Gail, 'it's not *not* an achievement. To be fair. She worked at it. Great surgery.'

Agata laughed with her mouth covered, like a geisha.

'You're far more naturally beautiful though,' Gail told her as Agata rolled her eyes.

'You are. You would be if . . .'

Agata's voice dropped. 'What?'

'Well, you would be if you were healthy.'

There was a long pause, the absurd din of the hockey players tossing the silence from one end of the field to the other, until finally:

'No.' Agata spoke as reasonably as any teenage girl ever has. 'I wasn't ever beautiful.'

Gail was insistent. '*You'll have changed since then.* But you won't know, because of all this.'

She motioned at the wheelchair.

'All what?'

'I'm sorry.' Gail spoke sincerely, now, measuring her question as she served it. 'You know you're sick, right?'

'Yeah,' said Agata, with a sigh, 'I know.'

'Isn't it . . .'

'*What?*' Agata flicked at the carer to leave and didn't nod her head at him until she considered he'd moved far enough away.

'Isn't it a bit boring living like this?'

Agata sat up in her chair, though it pressed against the bones of her back.

Gail kept pushing. 'Isn't hospital really very dull?' She could see the fear in Agata's eyes and added, 'That's been my experience.'

The attempt to gain her trust was sincere and manipulative at once. It wasn't a lie, but Gail fed it to her at just the right moment.

'Why were you there?'

'Oh,' Gail said, sounding pleased to have been asked, 'they put me there against my will.'

Agata could have cried. 'Me too.'

Gail didn't want her to cry – not yet – so she tried to rally her: 'You'd beat everyone here if you were healthy. Her,' she pointed at a hockey fiend with bulging calf muscles and boob sweat, 'and her. And your stepmum too.'

Agata met her eyes.

'Not that you need to beat your stepmum. Your dad has space in his heart for you both, but . . . I just think you'd be less bored if you were well. That's all.'

When a cheer went up, she momentarily forgot about the game and thought it was for her spiel. 'Was that OK to say, Agata?'

Agata had the pin prick of a tear in each eye but, from force of habit, she didn't swallow them back – she'd trained herself not to swallow, not even water.

'Yes. It's OK.'

'Can I ask you something? Do you count calories because you're bored? Or because you were angry but afraid of the anger? Was counting the calories like, meditation, calming down so you don't explode?'

Agata gripped the side of her wheelchair. The carer was looking at them as if he ought to be coming back. Gail took her swing, now or never. She crept close to the tormented girl and whispered:

'Be nice to be strong enough that if someone tried to hurt you, you could hurt them back. Instead of just hurting yourself all the time.'

'I like how it feels,' Agata said, quietly.

The sun was on their faces, warm, loving, uncomplicated in a way teenage girls secretly looked back on with a sense of bereavement. The moments when the warmth went behind a cloud and the chill set in made them sad for everything that had become clouded since high school. It was harder for Agata, since she was always cold, and though she had, with great intent and force of will, conjured a body state that would reflect her inner emptiness, the cold and the full-body shivers it unleashed made her feel as if she'd never had control of anything.

'Yeah. I get it. I've been there. It's addictive. None of them would understand, but I do.'

The carer was moving back towards them.

And she walked away before the carer made it to his charge, passing him. She felt Agata's eyes on her back as she walked the length of the pitch, the silly girls roaring behind her, the slap slap slap of the hockey puck, obscene like a porn overdub.

Ezra was waiting in the limo after school to collect Agata.

He saw Gail was holding the book he'd given her. 'Would you like a lift?' Agata asked her, smiling. Ezra was happy to see his kid smile but he was in no headspace to share physical space, especially not with *her*.

'It's about to rain,' she added, by way of explanation, for she could read her father and his displeasures.

He smiled through expensive, gritted teeth that could take more gritting and crumbled less than real ones. Gail didn't need to be asked twice, and got in. After she had settled herself into the limo she saw Faith pressing against the window.

'Goodbye, Agata! Hello!' she said to Ezra.

He nodded at Faith, but he didn't look at her. She was so very lovely that not to take her in exhibited the same willpower as not looking at a television that is on: even if she wasn't his type – if it's not on a channel you want – you look at it. But he didn't. Not at her long legs, not at her perfect hair. He sat on the seat opposite the girls, tapped on the divider and the driver took off.

Agata picked at her nails.

'Don't do that.' He regretted it right away. At least eating skin was eating. He'd told himself this grimly in the past when trying not to panic about her.

'Her stepmum does it too. She and her stepmother are very similar.'

'No, we aren't,' snapped Agata.

She was, in Gail's presence, not only speaking up more but being bolshier. He didn't like it, but could it really be bad? If her volume was higher, her batteries might not be dying?

'I think you guys are.' He turned to Gail, wanting her drawn in to the conversation so it might gain enough heft that Agata would have to keep talking. More kindling. He wanted to see her spark. 'They are two rosebuds growing from the same stalk.'

Agata sighed, theatrically. 'If you say so.'

He smiled. This was what a teenage girl was meant to sound like.

He wasn't ugly and he wasn't beautiful. But he did, with his upper lip covered again, look like a statue, like someone who had been here forever, the way Freddie Mercury and Cher did. He also had the best head of hair on any older man she'd ever seen. His down-curled lips would have been terribly unfortunate on a woman, but were ideal on a gangster turned 'businessman'.

'Do you have a favourite football player?' Ezra asked.

'It's hard to choose,' Gail said, his chauffeur eyeing her with ill-disguised irritation in the mirror. 'Terry Loft is very fond of you. Do you feel like Dad to your whole football team?'

Ezra nodded: 'His own country did not care about him. He came here without knowing anyone. And I think he's a real sweetie. That's why I have him at family functions. That's not for everyone.' He smiled. 'And the girls like him. You know what I'm saying?'

'Gross, Dad.' Agata had shrunken her sexual urges alongside her breasts.

'You saying you don't have a crush?'

Gail wanted to tell him to stop, that he'd undo the good work she'd done on the hockey pitch.

'Ezra, I didn't know who he was, I don't follow that stuff, but it's nice to meet someone that way, as a human, and not what the papers say about them. Let them have a clean slate. You know what I mean?'

'I think I know.' He winked. Why must British men sexualise everything? Idiots.

It was the first time she'd addressed him by name and even saying it in front of him felt like a provocation, as if he were too famous to be in the presence of his own name. The car felt it, absorbing the shock.

He looked at his daughter, as if he hoped she wasn't listening, which she wasn't.

'What does Gail mean?' he asked.

'It's from Avigayil.'

'What does Avigayil mean?' He was interested, even as he fiddled with his phone as if he wasn't.

'It's just from the Hebrew Abigail.'

'I know, but do you know what that means in translation?'

Gail was blank.

He stopped scrolling on the iPhone. 'You never looked it up?'

Gail looked uncharacteristically embarrassed.

She hesitated. 'It means "my father's joy".'

She knew it had been chosen so Dar could honour her own father, but it still stung. Everyone in the car saw Gail try not to cry and everyone looked away.

'I'm sorry,' said Gail, quickly mopping the wetness like a housekeeper to her own face. Ezra was disgusted by her apologising but also wanted to reach out and hug her. Finally, Gail, having stemmed her tears, asked, 'What does Agata mean?'

Ezra nudged his daughter. 'You know this one.'

Agata rolled her eyes. Her body was stymied but her eyes were very agile.

'It means "she who is virtuous".'

'When?'

'What?'

'When will she be virtuous?'

'Oy.' Ezra smiled. 'It's a fair point.'

'Some time in the future, I will. You're *so* funny.' But she enjoyed being teased.

'She's too busy on her phone. If she can have someone do the virtue for her via an app, she will do it,' he laughed. He felt in his bones, just as she did, that teasing her was a good sign, that he felt safe to do it. That he wasn't wrapping her in cotton wool. Father and daughter relaxed.

Gail had set it up for Ezra and he had delivered. She smiled shyly at him. But it was only faux shyly, which can come across like faux leather: the wrong texture and not appropriate on such a young girl – and he recoiled from the feel of it.

The girl had been helpful. She had done a mitzvah. And now she could go. You don't thank people for a mitzvah. You pay them for it. Ezra tapped his driver's head rest.

'Let her out here.'

'Here is fine,' Gail said, as lightly as she could, as if it had been her request. She'd learned this manoeuvre watching her mother.

The football fans were out in force, packs of them. She tried not to show her anxiety, pushing through them without looking any of them in the eye – seeing only the colours of their team shirts, like the colour trails before a migraine.

In the flat, she looked in the TV guide at what was on that night. Then she looked in her wardrobe. Then she looked in the fridge. And when she found something edible to take it with, she popped open her evening dose of medicine.

If she'd kept a ledger she'd have noticed that she generally wanted to write to George Michael two hours after taking her medication.

CHAPTER *14*

The first time Agata invited Gail over, just her, she never made it past the first floor. When Gail was let in by security, she saw Melody lying in the shag carpet in the living room, moving her arms slowly up and down, like she was making a snow angel. Melody looked at Gail dreamily as the girl walked in. She remembered her from the pool party, she thought, and said a friendly, 'What's happening?'

There was an illustration of a jumpsuit abandoned next to her, and a fountain pen with its cap hanging off, ink dripping into the soft fibres of the shag. Gail thought about helping but was transfixed by the sight of the ink as it spread. Melody was clearly high – so high – but Gail herself had never been high and it needed confirming.

'Hello, I don't think we really met last time – I'm Gail.'

'Gaaaaaaaail . . .' Melody sang.

'That's me,' Gail replied.

'Gail, I could eat inside you!' She said it with a true violence before collapsing into soft giggles.

Agata appeared and the girls looked at each other over Melody's body.

'Do you get the joke?' said Melody, from the floor.

'I think so, yes, the cafés with my name?'

'Yes, the cafés. They're everywhere. It's so comforting! They're on every corner to *offer succour*.' She made the two words sound obscene.

She turned her snow angel head up towards Agata.

'One day you'll eat properly again and you'll love it there, inside Gail's, eating inside Gail with Gail. It will be so powerful!'

Not noticing how this made her stepdaughter flinch, she began holding her jumpsuit design above her like it was protective glasses through which to view an eclipse.

'It's allll about fabric.'

But it was not all about fabric, not everything. Some things were, that was true. The way it had changed on Gail's body as she grew, the places it drew too much attention to and the ways she sought to hide it before relenting. How her mum bought her the wrong size bra, which cut into her flesh so it looked like she had four breasts or two segmented ones. But why didn't she buy her bras herself? Because she was sixteen and had no money. But doing it together was unbearable, her mother's hands on her shoulders as she turned her to look in the dressing room mirror. It was preferable for a mirror to reflect that you had four breasts and no mother's hands on your shoulders. Both were bad.

Gail had to admit that the illustration Melody was helicoptering in the tense air was well executed. She wondered if Melody had always been good at art and what attention it had brought her and where and at what age. Had there been a creepy teacher offering to nurture her talent? Had her teenage life improved or been scarred by his attention? She felt suddenly very sorry for her, in this entirely imagined trauma.

'Fabricccc,' sing-songed Melody, as if it were a prayer. 'It isn't white or beige, it's ecruuuuu.' It was now a meditation and seemed to help her drift off, her head going back down to the rug.

Lying flat, her multiple diamond earrings sparkling in the afternoon light, she beamed. 'I've always said . . .' But then Melody could not remember what she'd always said. And that didn't matter, because instead of passing out on a cold pavement like a football fan, she was safe at home.

Gail and Agata sat in the kitchen trying not to talk about what they'd just witnessed. Finding it hard, they parted ways abruptly before the tea had even boiled. The next day at school, Agata seemed to have been ruminating and was on edge, quite literally at the end of her wheelchair. 'Melody's mother died the year before last and she's still in mourning . . .' She didn't explain that high on pain meds was the easiest place to do it, but they both understood.

'She used to be so much fun, I honestly much preferred being with her to being with my mum. But now, we're shopping, she'll look at, like, a handbag and start to cry.' The bag Gail had seen her holding was tiny. She pictured tiny tears.

'That's sad,' said Gail.

'It's embarrassing. Crying there in *the* department store. The one he didn't get to have. Everyone knows who she is. Made it look like she was crying *about* it.' Agata shook her head. 'He's going to get it one day.' It was the first time Gail had heard her defend her dad.

'Of course, I know, I mean . . . do you think they're just antisemites?'

Now Agata's cheeks burned. 'Is that what you think?'

'Maybe,' Gail answered, nervous.

'Yeah, that's what he says. He said they did it to his father. It's a punishment. His dad changed his name so he wouldn't sound foreign and it wasn't enough. It will never be enough.'

Gail caught herself blushing at the thought that she and Ezra had come to the same conclusion, and she patted her pink cheeks to tamp them down, only making them redder.

'They have to smack Dad down for being too successful.'

Gail was just worldly enough to know that was certainly not the whole reason, but she tried to be gentle:

'Maybe we should all start going to synagogue together?'

'No!' Agata was angry now. 'That's the last thing he needs! To draw more attention to the problem.'

Gail felt a wave of frustration at the push-me-pull-you rhythm of their friendship. It felt like a dress rehearsal for a friendship, the jokes never quite landing, the actors waiting for their turn to speak rather than listening to each other. She understood and empathised that Agata had been sick so long she'd lost her understanding of how conversations even work.

'I just thought you might like . . .'

'Well, I wouldn't!' interrupted Agata. 'We're not like that. We're not religious. We don't want everyone to look at us like you do.' She was dwelling on the Parkers rejection, but Gail was the closest person to train her laser on. 'And why are you always following me around?'

Gail took a breath. This had been the problem with the last friendship. She'd come on too strong with Faith. The whole school knew. And in windows of clarity, she knew it, too. She understood she'd have to be more delicate this time.

Gail answered evenly, telling herself, *She's just hungry, that's why she flips like this.* 'I don't follow you around.'

'Yes, you do, every time I turn, you're there.'

'I'm just trying to help. I'm just trying to be helpful.'

'Go help someone else!'

'All right,' Gail answered. 'I will!'

The girls milling around looked up from their tuck shop wrappers and crush lists as Gail exited the school.

Making quick use of the lunch hour, Gail stormed up the hill to George Michael's house to see what he was doing, whether it was maybe time for him to walk his dogs. But the curtains were drawn and, without stopping, she merely said, 'I do not follow her around!' as she passed.

She walked back to school, and the storming downhill felt humiliating; storming downhill really took engaging your core completely all the way to not fall over. She tried to even her breathing, imagined neatly folding and putting away each exhale and inhale.

'Do you need help getting across the road?' she asked an old lady as she got to the zebra crossing, but she did not need help crossing the road. Gail realised, too late, that the lady was not that old, only her mother's age, and that she'd made her feel bad and strange. She paused at the creepy man's shop to get a Galaxy bar, huffing it like an asthma inhaler until she felt steady again, a Cadbury's Dairy Milk for later. You hadn't eaten two bars of chocolate in one day if they were different brands, was her logic. 'Aren't you supposed to be in school?' he asked, and she ignored him, which gave her a soupçon of her power back, tingling in the ends of her hair and tips of her fingers as she refused to be engaged.

When she got back to school, the bell for afternoon lessons had gone and she had to sneak in, which she did by hopping the gate near the caretaker's office. *Some security Ezra has implemented*, she thought, *ha!* Her class had started hockey and no one had cared that she'd skipped out on it since she usually did.

Agata was sitting on the sidelines, and she wheeled towards her, which was hard because her helper had gone to the toilet and the grass was bumpy. 'I'm sorry for what I said, Gail.'

'You don't have to be. It doesn't matter.'

'No, I am sorry. I'm just . . .' Agata's eyes widened. 'I think I'm just hungry.' The words tumbled from her lips, confusing her.

Gail understood the magnitude of what was being said and took another neatly folded-away breath.

'Agata. I knew that.'

'You did?'

'Yeah. Even when you were freaking out on me, I felt for you.'

'I'm sorry,' Agata whispered.

'It's OK, stop saying it now. But . . .'

Agata shivered with anticipation, praying on what she hoped would come next.

'Agata . . .' Gail considered holding her hand, then decided it would be more effective with space between them. 'Would you like one square of my Cadbury's Dairy Milk?'

Agata thought a long time. 'Maybe just one.'

Gail reached into her bag, unwrapped the chocolate bar, trying to be steady but anxious that if she took too long she might change her mind. Agata looked frozen.

'Do you want me to do it?' Gail asked.

Agata nodded and Gail placed it on her tongue.

Agata let the square of chocolate melt there a long time, and as it did, tears rolled down her face. Gail was very moved and whispered, as Agata sucked the sweet, 'I got you, I got you,' like she was an experienced man taking a teenage girl's virginity. 'I'm so proud of you.'

When the square was finished, Agata fixed her face.

Gail looked in her eyes.

'Would you like one more?'

Agata nodded, in a trance. 'Just a little bit more.'

CHAPTER *15*

Energised by the recent improvement in her stepdaughter's eating, Melody walked the aisles of Panzer's Deli. She felt like a useful housewife, as if she were in the American Midwest, as if the grocery bill wasn't going to be close to five hundred pounds here. She was sometimes trailed by Ezra's security when she went to Panzer's. Sometimes they saw something on the shelves they wanted, too, she could tell from their faces. 'Do you want that?' She'd back up. And they'd deny it, but she'd pop it in the trolley. She was good like that. It's what made her so likeable even as she was so oblivious – growing up hungry and poor, there were specific human behaviours to which she was highly attuned, things that only a teen who'd been both hungry and the focus of male attention could intuit.

The people working at the checkout at Panzer's were mainly Filipino – Melody figured if they weren't doing this job, in a few years they might be home helps to some of the elder customers. The staff at the patisserie stand out front were young and Jewish. They had piercings all along their ears, just like Melody, but done in metal, not diamonds. Melody found it hard to tell if they actually needed the job or if working here was a social thing, a way to chat with friends on a gap year.

She hoped Agata would develop this friendship. She'd try to help. She bought a few things for their next play-date. Double Stuff Oreos, Reese's Peanut Butter Cups – American imports were always exciting even if, like Melody, you'd now been there multiple times. The new girl would eat them, and Agata would eat half and then move it round her plate. And that was something new and ecstatic.

When she got back, Melody took great pleasure in arranging the provisions in the pantry, moving treats up and down on shelves as if weaving houndstooth. Gail's return to their home came soon enough. That weekend, thanks to a last-minute goal by Terry Loft, Ezra's team made the semi-finals. On Monday, Gail began wheedling.

The second bell for registration had not even gone when she said to Agata:

'It sounds like the next match will be fun!'

Agata made a face like she was biting into Ezra's Persian lemon. 'It's stressful. It's really not that fun.'

'I'm interested.'

Agata shrugged. 'I don't know why.'

Internally, Gail answered: Because, well, firstly it would be a brutal blow to Faith were she to be invited to attend. There might be a picture of Gail in the newspaper. And she wanted to talk more to Ezra. She had more to say to him. And, and, it would mean she'd overcome a fear of football implanted in her by Dar.

But she could sense she needed to tread carefully. She attempted, her words on tiptoes, another angle with Agata. Wouldn't it be *helpful* if she were there?

She could have approached Ezra when he collected Agata but it would have been awkward – she didn't yet feel she could count on Agata to set her up for the right shot. So ten minutes before class got out, Gail said she needed to go to the toilet. When she walked right through the gates, she imagined herself as Mikhail Baryshnikov in *White Nights*, defecting under cover of darkness.

She had already figured which way his limo would be coming from and was waiting on the right street. Helpfully, it started raining, so it was all the more effective when she 'accidentally' stepped in front of his car. His driver was swearing at her, the hostility she'd noticed from him before now blatant. He tried to stop Ezra from getting out to check on her, but he did it anyway, bending down in the rain and helping her up.

'Are you OK?' The driver took over and tried to lead him back to the pavement.

She nodded.

'Is school already out?' Ezra asked. 'Am I late?'

'No.'

'Then why are you out already?'

'They're trying to expel me,' she blurted. 'They're giving me to the end of the year before they decide.'

He was understandably confused. 'Because you walk out of lessons early?'

'Not really.' The rain was plumping her curls and her confidence. 'Maybe that's one of the things. They're making me come back before the Christmas holiday to tell me if I'm allowed to stay or not.'

He gestured around them. 'How the hell would bunking off help your cause?'

Instead of answering his question, she said, 'Am I going to be invited to the big football match then?'

Her voice was very clear, but he looked like he must have misheard, because he took a step back. So she added: 'I really want to, but when Agata asked me I thought I ought to check with you, in case she may have overstepped. I get that she's new here so maybe trying to get me to be her friend by offering something bigger than she should be. I'm already her friend. I don't need her to give me stuff. But if she wants me there I'll be there. I'm just checking with you.'

Her ankle was bleeding through her sock but he couldn't see that because of the length of her skirt. *The school bell will have rung*, she thought. She stood in a new way that hoiked her hem and he saw the blood. It seemed to flick a switch in him.

'You want to go to it?'

'It did sound fun when she asked me.'

'Then I will arrange it.'

Her blazer was now sodden in the rain. He handed her a business card.

'This is my direct line. Just in case you need it.'

Dear George,

When I got home, I took off my blazer and saw that my shirt was also wet, and that I looked like a teen girl in a pornographic image. He didn't see that though. But I did. I saw it. And it turned something in me, as the sight of the blood on my ankle had moved something in him.

Love
Gail

Dar and Gail ate dinner in relative silence, not least because what Dar had heated up was sticking to the backs of their teeth so all their energy was on chewing.

'Why don't you cook?' Gail said, finally.

Dar's head snapped up – she'd been deep in her own world. 'I do cook. I made you this.'

'You got this from a box. Why don't you know any old-world recipes?'

'You learn them!' Dar laughed. 'You learn them and make them for us.'

Gail stood up and made an ostentatious display of tipping the rest of her food in the bin.

In her bedroom, after she'd taken her evening medication, Gail retrieved the business card he'd given her and texted Ezra to thank him in advance for the ticket. She waited. There was not even the dot dot dot then retreat of a ghost, writing then deleting a response, which would sate her without him getting himself in trouble. But she saw that it had been read.

CHAPTER 16

It wasn't easy to get Agata to her stadium seat, even with her special place in the box. Ezra was talking a few seats away from them, a couple of executives between him and his daughter. Ezra had travelled separately to be with his team, telling himself they needed more than just his money. He believed they needed his presence before a match in order to power up.

'I'm so happy to be here,' said Gail, as she took her seat beside Agata.

She didn't say 'Thank you for inviting me' or anything else she could be called out on as factually incorrect. She fudged it enough that Agata – who did seem to know how unwell she'd been and that maybe therefore her memories might be hazy of what she'd asked of whom – let it slide.

She just commented, 'I didn't think you cared about football.' She had a thin voice and it suddenly occurred to Gail that it might get heftier once she gained weight.

Agata was correct: Gail didn't care about football. But she wanted to get close to the thing she'd always been afraid of, that Dar had told her to be afraid of.

The audience was more pleasant than she'd imagined, more *charitable*.

'This is a nice crowd actually, more how the crowd is at a ladies' match,' Agata whispered. 'Better class of fan.'

Gail looked over at Ezra, who was deep in conversation.

'Where's your stepmum?'

'She cooks a roast every Sunday. She gets really in a state about it and spends all day doing it. Doesn't matter if it's a match day.'

'Is she a good cook? Or is she the reason you stopped eating?'

Agata laughed dryly – no one else had tried making fun of her eating disorder.

'She doesn't cook, she thinks she does.'

'Sounds like a religious belief? Let her have it?'

She didn't recognise, right away, Terry Loft from Agata's birthday, since all the footballers had the same haircut. When he turned around and waved at them both, she sighed, irritated.

'Yeah, he's a pain in the arse,' Agata said. 'I said he had a cute accent a year and a half ago and now my dad won't let it go, like when you one time say you like ladybirds and your family keeps buying you things with ladybirds on them, like pillows and mugs and bracelets, because they don't really know you.'

'And the amazing part is your dad *literally* bought him.'

They laughed together and she thought she saw Terry look back at them, then realised he was looking at the coach for some kind of last-minute guidance.

Ezra leaned over to them. 'They're starting.'

Gail whispered to Agata: 'The coach looks like a really kind rodent . . .'

'Shhh!' said Ezra. She thought she'd been whispering but teenage girls don't have the best grasp of volume control.

'. . . like if he appeared in your sink,' Gail continued, 'he would ask if he could help you with the dirty dishes.'

She realised Ezra was glaring at her. Meeting his eyes, she used a coy, girlish voice to explain: 'I was just telling her . . .'

'You're the one that badgered to be here,' spat Ezra, 'now shut the fuck up and watch.'

Gail felt her heart drop to her stomach and her face turn bright red. He had barked at her in a way that made her physically jump. Dar never swore at her. The game began and as the players ran and swerved and kicked, she couldn't get herself back into her body. Ezra had sworn at her. And, worst of all, now Agata knew she'd forced her way in. As the game played out, she could barely watch, trying only to think what to do, how to compose herself and correct the course of the day. How to redirect the attention.

At some point Terry seemed to bump ever so mildly against another player, yet he fell to the ground, rolling on the floor, clutching his leg in anguish, his hat-hair immaculate despite his rocking back and forth on the grass.

The light began to dim, half-time came, and Gail found herself frozen to her seat with humiliation and anger. Agata finally started to notice something was awry and, prodding her, only got a hushed: 'Bit of a headache,' as Gail dug the nail of her right forefinger into her left wrist, pressing and pressing the mortification to get the thoughts in her head to, as Ezra said, 'shut the fuck up'.

The game resumed and when darkness fell and the floodlights came up, she suddenly understood her best course of action. She quietly reached into her bag, feeling for the object, which was meant to be carried with her at all times.

Once it was in her hand, she wiggled it out and tucked it behind her back. Then, lifting it (judging as carefully as she had when she'd fallen in the rain before Ezra's limo), she took aim. She waited, as if for the moment of silence near the end of a perfect pop song before the beat comes rolling back in – and then she let it happen: she dropped the bottle of pills, its cap already loosened. It fell to the floor of the stadium and the pills rolled down the steps.

'Oh, gosh!' she gasped.

Chasing down each pill, she crawled in front of Ezra. She pressed her ass in the air and stretched her waist long as she reached for the pills that rolled under his seat.

'For fuck's sake,' he said, and then, despite himself, 'do you need a hand?'

She looked up at him. His cheeks had flushed, blood visibly rising. She'd made his humanity come to the surface – that was something, that was a kind of power. Was he expressing anger? Shame? Who could tell? Red is red.

She reached for the last few pills and then located the cap.

Down on the pitch, Terry was catching his breath near their seats. He turned and smiled at her and ruffled his hair and mouthed, 'You again?' She made a face like the grinding teeth anxiety emoji and Terry turned back to the game.

She darted back to Agata, pressing her face into her bony arm.

'What? What happened?'

'I'm so embarrassed, I can't look at you.'

'What?'

'It was my psych meds I dropped. Now you'll think I'm crazy. Everyone in my family' (she didn't say it was just her and Dar) 'thinks I'm such a fuck-up. Like I cause all the friction when it would be that way even if I'd never got sick.'

'I know what you mean.'

Gail concentrated hard as she let her tears well. She let them and then she felt it happening anyway, without needing to concentrate.

'I'm really scared your dad isn't going to let you be friends with me now he's seen what's wrong with me.'

Agata's eyes widened.

'Fuck him! He can't stop us being friends.'

Gail sniffled.

'Really?'

'Really.' She pressed back into Gail, who smiled wanly and just then the crowd began to cheer.

A Mexican wave went round the stadium. She saw how anxious Agata looked at the prospect of crowd participation.

'Do you want to get out of here?' Gail said.

'Aren't you loving it?'

Terry Loft scored a goal and the crowd went wild, clutching each other, screaming and crying for everything they'd ever held inside.

'It's fun but you're more important. If you want to go, we go.'

'Yes, please,' said Agata. Gail made sure to look over her shoulder and mouth 'thank you' at Ezra as she pushed his daughter's wheelchair out of his match.

*

Next to the story about his team's unstoppable winning streak, there was a picture in the paper the next day of Ezra caught right as he'd been hissing, 'Shut the fuck up.' Nobody mentioned or asked who the hiss had been aimed at, promulgating the notion that it was just the normal face of a crass Jewish billionaire with a shady back story and bad manners. When Agata saw the photo over breakfast, she laughed and laughed and could not stop even when she tried, even when she saw her father's expression morph from quizzical to genuinely wounded.

CHAPTER 17

Gail could not remember anything from any school test, but she could remember every weekend that she spent at the Levy home. She'd sometimes arrive to find Melody arranging the pantry, talking to Gail, on seeing her, as if they'd been in the middle of a conversation.

The first time it happened, she thought Melody might have been confused, since she was looking back and forth between a newspaper review of her new-season collection and arranging rows of tea. On the counter, kugel ingredients had been laid out for her in advance to put together as if for a bright Montessori child.

She looked directly at Gail and asked: 'I mean, how can it be unwearable if I am, myself, wearing it?'

'That's true,' answered Gail, hedging her bets.

'He's having me work with old ladies in the East End.'

'Who, Ezra?'

Melody closed the pantry door. 'It can be really dangerous, working with family. We hired my mother as a nanny for Agata once and that was a disaster.'

'Her mother charged them!' explained Agata, backing away from the scents of the pantry and the past.

'Yes, but that's because Agata isn't my biological child.'
(She said it right in front of her.)

'I see.' Gail wondered how much longer this would go
on, when they could go up to the bedroom and be alone.
No time soon, it seemed.

'His aunties ran a corset shop in Whitechapel, been
there since 1890 – not them personally . . .'

'Of course.'

'And he thinks all these women have old-school tech-
niques for my gowns.'

Agata, needing this to end, enthused: 'I think it's a
brilliant idea. It would be upcycling taken to the next
level – re-using old ladies.'

'Oh, he said that! Now you've both said it, so I suppose
I must listen.'

'I think so.'

'Are you coming?' snapped Agata, having shapeshifted
to the exit, her tone and bones prominent.

The lift to her bedroom pulled shut like in a Joan Crawford
film and Gail wanted to reset her imagination for not having
thought up such a thing: a lift in a house! Not a stair lift,
but a real lift, with light-up buttons and interior cornicing.

Inside the lift, she felt unusually shy.

'I'd never seen a lift in someone's house before I met you.'

Agata shrugged. 'How many houses have you seen?'

Agata also had a separate living room attached to her
bedroom as well as an en-suite bathroom with its own
roof terrace.

'Do you want to go out there and smoke?'

Gail answered truthfully.

'I'd like to be photographed smoking, but I don't want to actually inhale. I did it one time and I vomited.'

Agata was delighted: 'I'm good at vomiting!'

'You must be very brave.'

Agata thought about it.

'I think I am actually. Thank you.'

She went over most weekends before school broke up for the summer.

Any time they were up there, listening to music, Gail always had one ear out for Ezra. She wasn't bored by Agata, but she did sometimes feel she was a stranger she'd been placed beside at a dinner party rather than a classmate she'd angled to befriend. The conversation was pleasant but slow moving and she watched the light beyond her window begin to ebb as they started to run out of words.

They moved on to decoupage, sitting on the floor, cutting pictures from fashion magazines and pasting them onto a board, like Peter Blake without a focus or point of view. Agata had a pair of Hermès scissors in her fingers and pillows under her bottom because it hurt her bones to be on the ground. The girls she was clipping out and glueing were just as thin but the camera had added ten pounds and you couldn't tell whether or not they also required soft padding to sit when they weren't being photographed for money. They were probably the same age as her. Gail got teary thinking how badly those girls maybe needed the money and whether anyone would help them manage it for college tuition.

Sometimes Agata would fall asleep on the fainting couch and Gail rode the lift back down to the family kitchen hoping to bump into Ezra or even Melody.

Melody was still upset by the poor review of her last collection. 'Sometimes I don't know why I do it. Or if I can keep doing it.'

'You can,' said Gail, always excited to be confided in, especially if it was by a member of this family. 'And you can go further. Collaborate with the old ladies. Stop being afraid. Stop thinking about reviews and the market. If you don't become the ocean you will be seasick for the rest of your life.'

Melody blinked at her.

'Leonard Cohen said that.'

'Oh, I *love* Leonard Cohen,' she blushed, the blood moving beneath her porcelain skin. 'I mean, that's obvious.'

'How?'

'Well, look who I married.'

Gail went through her head, Marianne, Rebecca De-Mornay . . . had Melody previously been married to Leonard Cohen? It was true that she was, like Marianne, a blonde, blue-eyed woman. But beyond that she was stumped.

'Did you guys play him as a first dance?'

'No. No! Ezra is my Leonard Cohen. He is so much like him. Don't you think?'

He was older. That was true. If he was soulful, Gail thought only she herself had been on the cusp of discovering it, way down beneath the surface of the vulgarity.

'Leonard Cohen wakes every day at 3am to meditate.' Gail tried to prod for a connection without pushing her away.

'No way! Ezra gets up every day at five.'

'Not to meditate.'

'We don't know that.' Melody put the kugel in the oven as Gail noticed the live-in chef hovering in the far corner of the room.

'I think we know that.' She adopted a tone of aggression as flirtation, as she'd seen Ezra do with Melody, how it seemed to soothe his young wife. 'Doesn't your husband get up every day at five to, like, wreak vengeance and decimate stock?'

'Oi! I heard that.'

He was suddenly there. Gail tried not to jump at having conjured him. Told herself it wasn't exactly a conjuring if they were already in his house.

'Well, don't you?'

'Oh, no,' said Melody, 'that's the villain in the tabloids. That's not the man I love, not at all.'

To be wanted by someone whose ancestors would have murdered his ancestors was very exciting to Ezra, even now. And Melody did look so good in her own designs. Not knowing how many great designers had been considered ugly or homely, a quarter of the height of his models like Azzedine Alaïa or obese like Christian Dior, he was happy to pump money into her clothes line, knowing she was the best possible advert for it.

Melody turned to Gail. 'What do you wear? The scent. I've been trying to put my finger on it since you first came here.'

'Oh. Just whatever is in my mum's bathroom.'

She knew exactly what it was and she wasn't going to tell. Saffron Troublant by L'Artisan and there was very little left of it. One day it would run out and she'd probably have to find a way to buy a new bottle for Dar's birthday. She didn't know a man had given it to her mother. She didn't connect the scent with romance or know how the wearing of it kept her younger lover present in the flat he'd only visited when Gail was at school and Dar had hours off work.

'I love perfume,' said Melody, 'I'm an absolute connoisseur so I will track yours down.'

'She will,' warned Ezra, taking a banana and walking out. Gail tracked him until he was out of sight. When he was gone and she could see she could not draw him back by will, she returned her attention to Melody.

'You should launch your own.'

'Me?'

'Your name on a perfume bottle? I think it's a winner. Your name is Melody – music and scent both being ineffable, hard to put into words or to contain. Scent burns off but music doesn't. A song is an ear worm, a scent you have to keep going back to huff. Do you know what I mean?' And though she'd never thought of it that way, Melody did know what she meant.

As they retreated to the drawing room, the chef waited a beat to turn the oven to the correct setting, moving the tray from the top grill to the bottom.

Gail headed home, knowing things had gone well and that she'd won Melody as a bonus. She felt elated on the top deck of the bus. She wanted to have sex. With someone. She wasn't sure who. One of the Levy family. Any of them would be worth exploring. She looked out over the Heath and envied George for not having to choose just one person.

When Ezra was ready, the family sat for dinner.

'Do you like it?' Melody asked as Ezra shovelled his kugel.

'It's beautiful. Better than my mother made.'

Agata had pushed it around the plate a few times before taking a single bite, then asked if she could be excused.

'I do like it.'

Melody rolled her eyes. 'But not enough to eat it.'

Ezra raised his hand.

'Let her go.'

Once they heard her in the lift, she continued: 'I know, I know, I just worked hard.'

'She worked hard too. Trust me,' he said. 'We are about to reach a breakthrough. With that girl here, she sat on her living room floor and ate half a bag of salt and vinegar crisps. For Agata, that's huge.'

'But so unhealthy!' Melody sighed.

'Who cares what she eats?' Ezra boomed. 'She ate something. *She ate something!*'

'I do think Gail is a good influence on her. I'm glad she went to St Saviour's. And she says the next thing I should focus on should be a perfume.'

'Wow.' He nudged his volume down. 'I think that's great. I'll have my people research the very best nose currently working.'

He sometimes forgot how deeply Melody operated according to who, what, when or where was nice or not nice to her.

'Yeah. Smart cookie, Gail,' he said. 'And she'll grow into her looks.'

'Oh. Yes. You'd have thought they'd have done rhino for her sixteenth,' agreed Melody.

This irked him. 'Not everyone is supposed to look like you.'

'You don't like how I look?'

'I love it. You're the most beautiful woman in the world. But Agata has a lot of me and I'm proud of that.'

Melody seemed agitated. 'Agata will have her nose done like everyone else?'

'Sure, of course. What are we, poor?' He paused. 'If she wants to and she's well enough.'

Gail couldn't bear to say she'd not been invited to stay for dinner. Instead, she attempted to transfer the bad feeling to her mother, needling her:

'Nothing you cook is ever fresh. Everything there is fresh.'

'They have a chef, I presume.'

'Melody made the most beautiful kugel tonight.'

'I thought you didn't eat there.'

'It *looked* beautiful.'

When Gail realised she was not only being an asshole but had the power to stop it, she did the thing where she forgave her mum, without Dar having actually done anything wrong.

She leaned in close and curled up on her and they watched a movie together.

'I've volunteered to accompany your class on the school trip to the National Portrait Gallery when you go back to school,' Dar murmured into the top of Gail's head.

'How come?'

'I happen to have the day off and it would be good for me to see the class and for them to see me.'

'OK, Mum. That will be nice.'

In the black-and-white movie people were dancing, not only light as air, but as if the wind were in their favour, suspending them aloft a beat before placing them gently back on the earth. Dar fell asleep on Gail, who tucked her in on the sofa.

*

'You still up?' she texted Agata from her bed.

'Ya,' came the reply.

'Did you eat the kugel?'

She watched the dot dot dot of the text being composed, like food being pushed around a plate.

'No. Gross.'

'You should eat the kugel.'

'You eat the kugel!'

'You're right. You could fill up on yoghurt?'

Agata considered this suggestion. In her head, slippery foods were something of a safe gateway. A part of her whispered that if you didn't bite into them, the calories would not be released.

'What was your mum like?'

Agata didn't need any beats to give a response. 'Weak. Dad paid her off. In exchange for me.'

'Do you hate her? Do you see her?'

'Nope. Sorry for her she's so weak. Makes me love my father more. He did that for me.'

'What about Melody?'

'Welcomed me from start. The one who gave me my name.'

'You didn't have a name before?'

'Yep. She gave me a better one.'

'What was it?'

'Never told me. Wanted fresh start, just us three.'

In the morning, on her way to school, she crossed paths with Dar in the kitchen and told her the story of Agata's name.

'That's extremely weird,' said Dar.

'Right?'

Dar poured her coffee.

'What else could be changed and when? No wonder that poor girl is so fucked up. What a mess they are. You've been very kind to her.'

'I'm trying.'

'She looks so boring. I know you're just being sweet because her home situation is so dreadful. I'm really proud of you.'

Dar leaned closer and closer to the balcony as she made her brutal declamation, so if a high wind had come, she could have blown off and it definitely would have been an accident.

CHAPTER *18*

It was a Saturday and Gail would ordinarily have been happy to have the flat to herself, would have sat in each room the way you do when you've paid for a nice hotel, have laid on each bed and turned around too so her feet were on the pillows. But Agata had gone away for the weekend with Ezra and the knowledge that she'd not been invited impacted Gail's ability to enjoy her empty space. So she wasted the time alone in the flat, eating it in one go without tasting it properly. She stayed in one spot all day, without even the energy to look through her mother's drawers. She did walk back and forth to the refrigerator, sucking in the cool and checking for food that she knew wasn't there but that she believed in.

Dar was on one of her marches – she didn't say she'd been hoping to spot him, still unable to process the possibility that he'd walked away from his beliefs in order to avoid her. When she saw he wasn't there, she ducked out twenty minutes before the finish line, as if it were an interval in a play she didn't understand.

She'd been tired of the other marchers in her bloc, no conversations left to have, the task at hand so gigantic and important to her and the conversation as they walked so banal. She had drifted over to a group of young South Asian men who scowled when she smiled at them. She didn't know how to react so she smiled harder.

'Is this funny to you?' a white man asked, aggressive.

'No.' And it wasn't, she meant it all, but a lot of women smile when they're hurt. She suddenly felt so far away from where she originated – both the desert land her dad had left all those years ago and the flat she'd left this morning.

She was ashamed of herself and, as a divine punishment, her feet hurt more than if she'd walked to the end.

Gail was eating the last yoghurt, her mother's special praline yoghurt, one of the only things Dar bought as a treat for herself. How long had she been waiting with the container in her hand, so that Dar could get home to see her finish it?

She wasn't up for Gail's bullshit and tried to tuck her banner away as quickly as she could. But Gail was too quick. She pointed her spoon at Dar.

'Who came first? I mean, if you google it, and the internet doesn't know you have an opinion either way, what's the, like, archaeological answer?'

'Well, the Jews were living there first, but that's only because . . .'

'Yes?'

'Yes, it's only Islam hadn't been born yet.'

She saw the smile curl across her daughter's face like a fortune-telling cellophane fish from a joke shop.

'But it's not like that. Their ties were deep, they'd been there long enough to consider it their homeland and the Jews had been gone so long . . .' she stammered, trying to flatten the cellophane to point to a different outcome. Even if the fish was a trick, a trick still has power over you.

'Because they'd been exiled . . .'

'Well, yes, but . . .'

Dar sat down, crushed. She could never win with Gail, never. It was devastating, as painful as having given birth.

'If,' Gail ostentatiously licked the spoon, 'they both have such deep ties to it – one of them was there first and the other was there more recently – why can't they share it?'

'Oh, Gail! You think that hasn't been asked?'

'Oh, *sorry* for asking something that's already been asked!'

But she stared at her mother, daring her to answer.

'That's naive. We are safe here. And in Brooklyn and Florida and California. We're not going to get kicked out of anywhere ever again.'

Gail raised her brows. 'St Saviour's wants to kick us out.'

'*That's* not going to happen either.'

'What if it does?'

'Then something better is waiting.'

Now Dar sat down on the sofa and beckoned Gail over, who very reluctantly followed, deliberately placing a paisley cushion between them. With this cushioning, Dar asked as delicately as she could: 'Do you feel about Agata the way you felt about Faith?'

'What are you?' Dar had wanted to ask, to tell her life would be easier if she were just gay and just said it. There'd be so much support.

Gail could never tell her it was the father she was fixated on, any father would be an issue, *he* would be . . . she'd considered using it to her advantage, aware how it would rupture her relationship with her mother, maybe even irreparably.

Gail ignored her, got up and fussed with the blind.

'Gosh, it's hot,' said Dar, politely acknowledging that the conversation was over.

'You'd have been rubbish in the desert,' Gail said, churlish.

Dar was annoyed. Gail was asking too many complicated questions, she couldn't be placated with black-and-white movies. And she couldn't shake the feeling that all Gail's questions about why two desert tribes couldn't live side by side were really about having to share a top-floor flat with her.

Agata hadn't replied to Gail's last few texts, she could see they hadn't even been read. She forced herself to leave the flat, stomping the pavement, shaking out her bad feelings. But with each step, she fell deeper into imagining what their father-daughter activities might entail, picturing their bonding expeditions to galleries and ice-cream parlours. In her head, Agata would point at a sculpture that moved her and Ezra would be so overwhelmed with pride and a sense of connection that he would secretly have the sculpture waiting at home for her return. Each day they'd sit beneath it, cross-legged, and confide in each other. The images came to Gail in such sharp focus, the laughter between the father and daughter so vivid, she suddenly wondered if she had been too cross with Dar to remember to take her medicine. She was too cross to remember. Dar texted her to come home.

Once Dar had started texting Gail, she could never stop, like a bag of sweets that could not be tasted properly until she reached the final one. The final one, the one she could actually taste, was when her daughter responded. Her daughter did not respond.

Gail walked and walked. As she approached George Michael's road, she stopped and looked.

She wanted to ring the bell but hadn't the nerve. And say what? She knew she mustn't, even if she was close to the end of her tether. Instead she sat on a bench in Pond Square and wrote a letter. Dar called and Gail let it ring out. Sitting in the square was in a way like being inside a contained space with George.

(The sky was still so bright, too bright. The birds were chirping off key, challenging music that kept one ear alert, 'Wake Me Up Before You Go Go' run through the dissonant songs on *The White Album*.)

She wrote George a letter somewhat shaped by her vivid imaginings of Agata and Ezra, acknowledging how intimidated he must have been (growing up a gay boy) by his father's macho interpretation of fatherhood. How imperiously the immigrant restaurateur carried his role as head of the family. How had that fear of his father been mended or exacerbated once he had accrued so much more money than him? Then who was the head of the household?

To her horror, when she put her envelope through the letter box, a sound immediately buzzed and she thought touching George's mail slot had set off a security alert, or maybe a very specific and high-tech alarm set off by letters invoking fathers. It took a moment to realise it was just Dar texting again.

As she walked back towards home, the sun had finally set (summer sun always reluctant to leave the stage). She stepped over each new text in the dark. Eventually she came to one elegant house, four storeys tall, whose windows were marked on the outside by burglar deterrents. But from the inside, between thick, heavy curtains made of damask silk, was a placard against the glass:

JUST STOP OIL

She wondered if it was the work of one person, alone with her moral compass, or if it was the work of a family who all felt the same way. She wondered if the family, despite their shared beliefs, had bickered as they put it up, accusations of mis-centring and whether to use Blu Tack or tape. Had they ever been on a march and had they met her mother at any of them?

But her brain wasn't working well. She hadn't taken her medicine. She knew that now. She should get home as fast as possible, but she was rooted to the spot.

Turning, she saw, parked in the driveway of the home, a vintage Mercedes and on the back of it a bumper sticker reading #GirlDad.

The feeling of rage roiled as she squeezed her eyes shut.

'They're just trying to be good people,' she said out loud.

Dar texted again and when she looked at her phone she saw not the message apologising and asking to meet at home, but #GIRLDAD now in text form, inside her phone. Without thinking, she took her phone and threw it through the window of the house in front of her. The glass shattered and a siren went off and she immediately wanted her phone back as much as she wanted not to have done what she'd done, and suddenly she was extremely sober with no aural or visual hallucinations.

Because it happened in this particular neighbourhood, maybe even because it happened close to a celeb-
rity home, the police car pulled up quickly. This was
neither here nor there, since she hadn't moved, just stood
there wondering if she could climb into the house for
her phone. She could hear, even now, over the alarm,
the sound of her mother ringing her. But how could
that be?

'Do you hear that?' she asked the policewoman as she
emerged from the vehicle. There was already a guy in the
back seat with his hands in cuffs. He was an older man
with buzz-cut grey hair and a moustache. Gail leaned
forward and asked him:

'Do you hear that?'

'Stay where you are,' warned the policewoman. 'Can
you tell me what you've had?'

Gail closed her eyes before answering.

'I've had a yoghurt that belonged to my mother.'

The policewoman sighed.

'Let me call your mum, I reckon you don't want me
calling your dad.'

'I'd love it if you could call my dad. I don't have one.'

'You're probably better off that way,' said the man in
the back of the car.

Gail agreed with him, as the woman touched her head
gently to guide her into the back of the car beside him.
Now she examined him more closely, realising their prox-
imity to the Heath and the fall of night.

'Cottaging?' she asked him, saucer-eyed. He nodded.

'Do they still pick men up for that then?'

He nodded again, like a sage saving his best words.

'That's crazy.'

She turned to the policewoman at the wheel and saw a male police officer in the other seat. So they did work in partnerships.

'That's crazy,' Gail repeated.

The policewoman answered, 'If it makes you feel better, you're in more trouble than he is.'

But he had handcuffs and she didn't, so Gail reached forward and tapped her shoulder.

'Are you going to put me in a cell?'

'No.' The policewoman was tired. So tired.

'Listen: I was only posting a letter to George Michael. That's not a crime.'

The male officer perked up. 'Depends what was in the letter.'

Gail had to hold back tears. 'My hope to guide him if he needed guiding and maybe my own aspirations.'

'That's not a Class A offence,' the cruiser offered.

Gail turned to the cruising man. 'Can you persuade them? That I'm not well but I'm not high.'

The man leaned nearer her face, studying her before agreeing: 'She doesn't look high, her pupils are fine.'

'Do you know George Michael?' she whispered to him.

He rolled his eyes. 'Do you work for the papers?'

'I'm just a schoolgirl. I'm seventeen in a month.'

'I wouldn't put it past them, the way they hound him.'

'I know!' agreed Gail, volume unmodulated, 'I know! It's not fair. None of it.'

Eventually parked outside the flat, the policewoman said there wouldn't be charges pressed. There was nobody home at the time of the vandalism, thankfully, as they were in their second home in Cornwall for the summer.

Before they parted and Gail rolled into bed as if nothing had happened, all four of them in the car agreed that the papers were disgusting and that George was a lovely man who deserved to be left in peace.

'Not my type though,' said the kind cottager, wrinkling his nose with distaste. 'Too foreign.'

CHAPTER *19*

She was more careful about her medication as the sun blessed them and her opportunities within the Levy house expanded. Given that Gail had only been in their orbit a few months, she was surprised and delighted to be invited to Melody's birthday. Not invited to her birthday *exactly*, but over for a date with Agata on the day it was Melody's birthday. It didn't feel small and it made up for the weekend they'd taken away without her.

When they let her in, Melody was admiring a new Hermès Birkin bag Ezra had given her with a painting on it, as if the leather were a five-pound canvas from the art store. *What do the imperially wealthy buy as gifts?* she thought. Invaluable things to render worthless.

The girls hung out in the TV den, watching old episodes of *The Fresh Prince of Bel Air*. Gail couldn't have concentrated on anything with a plot, not while she was trying to get a sense of whether Ezra was in the house without actually asking. Agata laid a bare foot on Gail, and Gail said nothing, just started gently pulling each one of her toes as if playing with a baby.

She had reached the littlest piggy when, from the kitchen, they heard a kerfuffle – more angular than that, a shrieking. When they got there, they found Melody pointing, mouth agape, at the gift she'd just unwrapped, while Ezra squeezed her waist, asking, 'Do you love it? Do you love it?'

There were two empty champagne flutes on the counter. Gail moved closer to the source of Melody's astonishment. Revealed inside pink tissue paper, framed in gold, was Marilyn Monroe's certificate of conversion to Judaism.

'From when she married Arthur Miller,' Ezra said. 'I picked it up at Christie's a while back but tucked it away for today.'

Gail wanted Marilyn's certificate more than she'd ever wanted anything.

'He gives great birthday gift,' cooed Melody, and, turning her neck upwards, kissed him deeply.

Then, without removing his arms from around Melody's waist, Ezra reached out his leg and tapped Gail on the foot with his foot, saying: 'Stick around and you'll see.'

Gail called home and said she had been invited to stay the night with the Levys.

Dar rarely had a night off and she was hurt. She'd taken time off work specially in order to accompany them on the school trip to the National Portrait Gallery.

'But the school trip?'

More champagne was being poured and even Agata had drunk a few sips. Gail wanted to get off the phone.

'I'll meet you there, Mum.'

Dar hung up and sat on the armchair set up at the window with the most expansive view, a framed portrait of her father set beside it. It was only 8pm and the flat was hers for the night. It wasn't like she could call someone to come over. Well, she *could*. But it had been a long time and would be a bad idea. Who knew if he still had the same number? He'd stopped coming to the embassy protests entirely, even though Palestine hadn't yet been freed. Someone who'd given up their entire belief system just to avoid you isn't going to take your call just because it's been a while.

CHAPTER 20

When Gail and Agata were let out of the limo, Dar was waiting at the school gates with a Thermos of coffee in hand. She tried to look through the tinted window to see if it was him in there, but she just saw shadows.

There had been a discussion before Ezra and Melody fell asleep the previous night about whether or not Agata ought to attend – not whether she was strong enough, because everyone could see how she'd improved, but whether she should have security, and concern about manoeuvring the wheelchair. In the end they took Gail at her word that she could manage the wheelchair without the carer.

Emerging from the car, Gail waved distantly at her mother, as if she were a royal and Dar a factory worker.

They'd been dropped off only just in the nick of time, so all the other students were already lined up to leave for the Tube. Faith visibly blanched on seeing the two girls exiting the limo together. Well aware of their history, Dar attempted eye contact with Faith, an act of connection, but Faith wouldn't have it. She avoided Dar's gaze as much as her daughter's.

The other parent there, as they walked two by two along the pavement, was a dad she had not seen before and had no interest in getting to know. He made a great show of being a dad volunteer, as if he ought to be commended for crossing some grand gender divide. She wanted neither to congratulate him nor make small talk. He had brought a large red Thermos and she practised in her head what she'd say if he offered her any of its contents. As they reached the station, a young female teacher scuttled from side to side like a useless crab whose days, through lack of evolutionary skills, were clearly numbered.

Dar had pictured something else in her head when she'd signed up. What did she *think* would happen on a school trip? That her daughter would cross sides to be with her, that a mass of strangers would bear witness to their allegiance? That they'd move through the gallery, lost in their own world, as they discussed each picture? That they'd look, heads together, like a portrait to be hung there? The mistake had been easy to make – in every other facet of her life, volunteering had enhanced her sense of self.

Agata seemed astonished by the train and embarrassed by the wheelchair. Dar tried to help Gail help Agata manoeuvre herself onto the carriage but Gail snapped at her mother in the tone Ezra had snapped at her during the football match. Dar hung back and stayed away.

On the train, as they rumbled between stations, Gail made eye contact with Agata, perfectly still and watching her own reflection in the window, the girls running wild around them. She leaned down as silently as a jaguar in a tree and whispered in her ear: 'You're done with this chair now. Aren't you?'

Nodding, watching herself nod in the window, Agata agreed that she was.

Transfixed by the two girls' intimacy, pressing her hands into the worn, discordant fabric of her seat, Dar strained to hear what they were saying.

'You're going to start walking again before this day is done,' whispered Gail.

Agata didn't answer but let the thought swirl inside her mouth like a forbidden taste.

Dar's hearing, like her mind, was not at its best today. She was so tired.

And the shrieking of the girls! The noise and stress of a hospital shift was bearable compared to this sound, or was it just that she was used to being with Gail alone? Gail had stopped bringing friends home when puberty hit. Dar hadn't minded. She liked their time together. But since she hadn't been around the girls en masse she only saw, now, how different her daughter was around them. Her voice had a stridency, a lack of control.

At the gallery, Dar couldn't help tracking the male eyes watching the girls as they tore around the rooms. 'Dial it down, girls,' she said, affecting cool, as if, collectively, they were a pop record she wasn't that into, their synchronised shrieking a wall of sound. How could anyone stand being around teenage girls? The Tudors on the walls looked suitably pissed off.

They each had a little trail booklet to follow, which they were mostly ignoring, bar Lilah who annotated hers diligently.

In the cafeteria, the other dad tried – as she'd feared – to make small talk but quite soon got the message and kept his chat and his Thermos to himself, looking at her coldly when she asked if he might watch everyone while she went to the ladies' room.

'Take some with you,' he huffed.

She had a few of the girls accompany her to the stalls. While running the taps, Dar tried to snatch a look at her face in the mirror, arrange a lock of hair, but she saw that they'd caught her, the teenage girls, and she blushed and dried her hands.

They moved on to the making of modern Britain, eminent figures like Riz Ahmed, Mick Jagger, David Hockney and footballers Gail didn't recognise but imagined Ezra owned. This was the first sliver of his presence. Agata breathed a sigh of relief that there was no portrait of him hanging (she wasn't sure if one existed and didn't know what she preferred, the idea that he hadn't merited a sitting or the fantasy that her father was being held in storage).

Agata had genuinely forgotten what was coming next, so profligate had his donations been in the last decade.

Gail wheeled her around the corner, and there was her father's name across the entrance to the entire inter-war wing. The letters were carved in the Roman style, but he had chosen that particular space because it was so British. Agata spotted his name and whispered, 'Wheel fast.' When she felt no one was looking, Gail brushed her fingers across the eye-level plaque for the blind bearing his name in raised braille.

Dar was a step ahead of the shoal and strides ahead of the useless crab-woman teacher as she led them into Great Women.

She'd only just locked eyes with Malala Yousafzai when she found herself confronted by a different sight, one that made her stagger back as if shot. A young man – maybe twenty-eight or twenty-nine – was kissing a woman she took to be a few years younger than him. For a second, her brain told her she was looking at a picture, rather than at two real humans. But Dar knew right away it was him from the shape of his skull, from the Hokusai waves of hair round the nape of his neck.

When she had thought, from time to time, of their reuniting, of him seeing her again, it was never like this, with his arm around the waist of a young woman, and she the stern, under-slept guardian of a gaggle of girls.

The woman he now moved his arm around was fashionably dressed and pretty, and Dar saw the St Saviour's girls looking at her with admiration. It was watching them watch her that tripped Dar up. Before she could move past, eyes averted, he saw Dar, blanched and quickly looked away.

For the rest of the trip, she stumbled from room to room, disconnected. She was not herding them correctly and they began to spread along different wings of the building like tentacles. The useless teacher and the Thermos dad corralled them as Dar leaned broken against the wall until a security guard asked her not to. Through the prism of her lashes and the prison of her heart, she saw the young man hustle his young love towards the exit.

Unaware of why her mother had dropped back, but relieved by it, Gail pushed Agata in her wheelchair along a marble hall, giving the chair a shove and letting go so she could spin. 'Wheee!' Agata sang, joyful. They did it again and again, Crab Teacher and Thermos Dad incapable of stopping them. Finally the same security guard who'd admonished Dar stepped in, speaking harshly. But Thermos Dad rushing forwards, pointed to Ezra's name on the wall and then at Agata, and the security guard hung back.

And then, when faced with a tight corner that would not allow her wheelchair the space it needed, Gail bent towards Agata.

'Now,' said Gail.

Agata shook her head. 'I don't think I can.'

'I know that you can.'

Agata got up and walked. She got up and walked right across the gallery floor that bore her name above it.

Wobbly as Frankenstein's monster, she turned to Gail and smiled.

On the train back to school, Agata's wheelchair had been folded up. She was sitting in a real seat next to Gail, while Faith feigned having absolutely no interest in them, even though she had positioned herself within a group of girls sat directly opposite.

Crab Teacher and Thermos Dad were talking about Agata's incredible breakthrough, Gail having attained a messianic aura right there in the middle of rush hour. Several girls had recorded the pivotal moment on their phones.

Dar sat slumped on her own. The vision of the beautiful boy she'd loved, with his arm around a woman his own age, haunted her, as if he were seated opposite her with the girl on his lap. And still the girls squealed, that terrible wall of sound. What happened next came as suddenly as a train derailment.

'Just shut the fuck up!'

Thermos Dad snapped his head up. The other passengers snapped their heads up too. Dar was so appalled by what she'd done that instead of stopping, she kept going.

'Just shut the fuck up, all of you. You selfish little shits. There's other people in the world, too, you know.'

The other people in the world turned their heads away from her, as they did from any unhinged older woman swearing on public transport.

Gail, who had been so furious she could not even speak until they were back at the school gates, said she would be staying with Agata that night.

'I was trying to do something nice for you, Gail.'

'How was that supposed to be nice?'

'Because I don't get to be part of school stuff usually. Because I'm always so busy with work.'

'You should have asked me. You could have asked me if I wanted you to be there and I'd have told you NO. If you'd told me you were having a mental breakdown I'd have said, "Don't come"!'

'I'm not having a mental breakdown.' Dar wondered if and how soon the event would get reported back to the headmistress and how it would affect Gail's chances of being expelled before Christmas.

'I'm going to Agata's.'

'You should probably ask her parents first.'

'They're expecting me. They feel sorry for me.'

When she got home to the empty flat, Dar sat in her chair with the view and her father's portrait by her side and cried and cried.

Her father had never cried in front of her and had rarely cried at all. He said he had protested when the policeman confiscated his watch from his wrist, as they had his brother's, on charges that they were spy radios to the Zionists. He protested but didn't cry and, somehow, he was one of the lucky ones permitted an escape. Maybe because he had held it together with such an absence of emotion. He didn't cry when security beat him when he left Iraq, the only country he'd ever known, his beloved country.

He did cry, finally, in Tel Aviv, looking at the other survivors who'd witnessed the desecration of their towns and seen the bodies of their families, the ones arriving, barely human, from Europe. Until he saw them, he hadn't understood that this fervour was everywhere, he'd been so trapped in his own horror. He said he cried then, because empathising with their pain was less traumatic than making any sense of his own.

That night, at Agata's, as desperate as she had been to get away from Dar, Gail felt a deep well of sadness. It was a sinking feeling that she'd made her mum walk to the well of sadness all alone each day to provide for them, when she could have been helping her. She knew that she should correct this. Agata snored lightly, a metronomic sound for a writer to compose to. She wanted, in that moment, to let Dar know that she saw her as a complex human with her own needs. But she feared that if she unlocked that, she might misplace the key. So she did the next best thing.

Dear George,
I know you have gone downhill since your mother's
death. I know she was the glue that held you together. I

envy you this. My mother is the glue, but she gets on my fingers and then I put my fingers in my hair, and then my hair looks not how I meant it to look, but somehow it's now the way she always said I should wear it and would be most flattering to my bone structure. Or I am feeling good about her being the glue that holds me together, it's making me feel warm and safe and held, and then I accidentally touch my eyes with the glue and it all becomes frightening. Obviously, I have to go to hospital because of the glue, but since she works at the hospital, I have to be on her territory to get fixed for what she's made me do. Everyone who knows her says, 'Oh, your mum is so proud of you, she's always talking about how close you are,' while I'm sitting in the waiting room, injured. So I leave. I'll live with her being the glue I got in my eyes even if it means I don't think I'm seeing things properly because of her. I don't think that's how it was with your mum.

All of this is to say, I should treat her better, I guess, like you did, because one day I'll be bereft the way you are. So, yes, it's all to say, if I can help in any way in your time of trouble. Just be an ear.

Love,
Gail

Agata stirred and Gail sealed the pages away. She felt a little window of understanding in that pre-dawn light that this was someone else's family, not hers. It was a window opened just slightly, but she felt in her bones a draught. She pulled the blankets so tight against her it was like she was back in the womb.

PART 4

CHAPTER *21*

It had been at the start of the summer holiday when Ezra caught the closing door of the lift with his hand, stopping her as Gail was headed up to Agata's bedroom.

'I heard what happened on the school trip,' he said, cocking his head.

She rolled her eyes beneath black lashes. He clocked, for the first time, how long they were.

'About my mum losing her mind?'

He stepped into the lift with her, the doors closing, amplifying her scent.

'About Agata walking.'

His brain caught up and he heard what she'd said.

'What do you mean? What happened with your mum?'

She shivered with delight at having captured his interest. The flat she lived in with Dar accentuated their issues because it was too small, but here, in the lift, the walls helped expand her way into Ezra.

'She lost it on the Tube. She shouted at us, she swore and told us all to shut the fuck up.'

He laughed: 'A woman after my own heart!'

'You can have her.'

'Hey! Don't talk about your mum like that.'

'She's not a perfect Jewish mother like I guess yours was.'

'Mine wasn't perfect. She was scary. She was proper frightening.'

He was so assiduously pushing his mother out of his mind, he hadn't actually meant to step inside the lift. But he did it, the doors closed and suddenly the air between them was electric, like they could kiss, maybe, but also more than that, like there was a good chance they might plummet.

'I punished her by putting her in the second-most expensive care home instead of the most luxurious. Which was smart since this one' – he pointed at the sky as if Agata was not up in her room but in heaven – 'has ended up costing me an arm and a leg.'

'Is your mum still alive?'

'The bills say "yes".'

She took a step forward.

'You smell nice.'

'Thanks,' he answered, cool.

'Don't you think it's interesting that Melody smells of gourmand scent?'

'What do you mean?'

'She always smells of vanilla or rum. Of fattening things.'

He knew that Melody hated earth scents. They made her think of her grandma digging potatoes in Poland. And that she loathed the independent perfumers with their abstract smells – 'wet grass' or 'fresh laundry' or 'library'. It was funny the things you could get angry about when you had everything.

'Yeah. Why are you telling me this, who cares?'

'Because Agata has had so much trouble with food. It's interesting that her stepmother would do that.'

His face went red like it had at the football match. 'Fuck's sake.'

'What? What did I do?' stammered Gail.

'Who says that out loud?'

'Sorry. I just feel comfortable being myself around you.'

He put up his hands. 'Well, you shouldn't.'

He pushed the button and the lift started moving.

'Well, Gail.'

Even though she'd made him mad, she liked hearing him say her name.

'I'm very happy about what happened.' He calmed down, remembering why he'd followed her in. 'About the walking part.'

'Oh, you're welcome. I knew that she could do it,' she said. The doors opened.

'Yeah. I guess I didn't.' He shrugged. 'Nice to be surprised at my age.'

She turned before he was gone, turned fast and, when she replayed it in her fevered mind, wished she'd done it slower. 'How old are you?'

He screwed up his face. 'You can google that.'

'Oh, yeah.' Did he know she already had? Was he a shrewd judge of character? Was that how he'd made it all the way here? All the way to a home with a lift his daughter could take to the top floor? The truth, though he would not like to admit it, was that he had once been a great judge of character, but that his judgement had become dulled, the edges softened by money as surely as it would have by alcohol.

With his door sealed, he sat at his desk, a pile of documents to read, a possible second shot at Parkers – but he couldn't focus.

He had wondered about Gail – not whether she was a literal spy from an industry competitor or a foreign government. But it had crossed his mind that she was a Jacobean spy, playing the court off against each other. And then Agata started to get better and he was able to throw himself back into having a real family. Where he had, until this miraculous demi-recovery, felt unable to throw himself into anything, only to slide under the cracks of doors in search of slivers of light, dirtied by her madness, by her silence. He who was so loud, the life of the party, wrestling with his daughter who had spent years stealing all the silence in any room.

There had been a particularly bad day, before she was at St Saviour's, when Melody knocked on his door and told him it was time to go to visit Agata at the hospital. And he'd simply said, 'I don't want to see her right now.' 'But she needs you,' Melody had replied. 'Maybe, but I'm angry at her.' Melody had made a face and he'd snapped, 'Calm down, I'll see her. But not yet. Right now I'm too angry and that's fine.' (The doctor had said that wasn't fine and so Ezra cut off the treatment and moved her elsewhere. Melody raged at him that night. Agata would have been touched at how hard her young stepmother fought for her that evening.)

Ezra had waited until his wife had finished berating him. Then he took her Prada bag from her shoulder and placed it on the dresser, then unbuttoned her fur and hung it on the hook, the unspoken threat that he had given her these things and he could take them all away. Melody went very quiet and went to sleep in her own quarters, slipping back in to retrieve her handbag. She trod ever so carefully so he wouldn't see, and he didn't see because he was no longer in his bed, having left the house to visit Agata after all.

They'd knocked her out. Her veins were purple and green, ill matching, she should have just had one colour vein, it was too much, in her silence her skin was too noisy. He moved closer and saw for the first time that there was a soft patch of downy hair sprouting on her back. It was beautiful and disgusting. It made him think of sex, the way it could be both those things, and he wanted to leave as soon as possible.

Instead, he made himself pass fifteen minutes watching her sleep – and his security watched him watch her sleep – and he didn't send him away, because he wanted a witness to how much he loved his daughter, to the fact that he was a great dad. This guard would surely tell the other people who worked for Ezra. That was how good feelings started. Not from above. He gently kissed his daughter's forehead before he left.

On her last night in that particular hospital room, Agata opened her eyes around 3am, when all the hardest thoughts move in. But she felt a strange peace. She looked across the water at the London Eye, knowing exactly what it felt like to move at such tiny, incremental intervals that no one could catch you doing it.

He gave up with the Parkers papers on his desk and, checking she was somewhere else, went into Melody's bathroom. The bathroom was epic, so he wasn't completely sure where to look. But he found her scent bottles in a glass medicine cabinet. She liked to have them on display. She liked to see as well as smell them. He opened each as delicately as his thick fingers would allow, and carefully smelled each one, then when he was done, instead of returning them to their rightful place, he took all the gourmand scents – the vanilla and rum, the pistachio, caramel and chocolate notes – back into his office and locked them in his desk drawer.

It took Melody only until bedtime that night to notice because she used a different scent at night than she did during the day.

'It must have been the housekeeper,' he said, perplexed, and Melody let her go the next day. He wasn't there to see it happen, but he'd known that it might and that it was deeply, deeply unfair.

Then it was the weekend and people were coming over for supper and Melody needed the house cleaned but there was no one to do it.

'Now what?' she sighed, putting her head in her hands.

'You tidy it,' he said.

'What do you mean?'

'You do the housekeeping today. You're young and healthy.'

'I'm a designer.'

'Yeah? The financial results say otherwise.'

She flinched and pulled away, went into her bathroom and reached for a pill from the top shelf of the cabinet in order to get through the dinner party.

He never spoke to her like that. For her he had endless patience. What was happening to them?

CHAPTER 22

At the start of August, the Levys went to Sardinia for two weeks, the girls texting each other every day, the separation exacerbating their emoji ardour. Counter-intuitively, they never had by text the aggressive back and forth they sometimes had in real life.

On their first night home, Agata and Gail were watching a movie together and thinking up ways to spend the October half-term and what they might do for Gail's seventeenth birthday that weekend. The tan Agata had returned with covered her face, neck and arms, but not her lower half, which she'd kept covered on the yacht. It was like she'd returned as the ocean itself: the places where it's warm dropping suddenly to cold. Because of her low body weight, Agata had got used to falling asleep very easily, and it was a habit that stuck even after she had gained a significant amount back.

A floor down in the living room that led off from her bed chamber, Melody herself was drowsy. She was still on pain meds from a minor cosmetic procedure, which would neither be named nor, she hoped, noticed but which she'd found an immediate opening for after Ezra had spoken to her so harshly. The accompanying opiate had, as it always did, given her what she called 'the spendies'.

Once Agata was asleep, Gail wandered down and knocked on her door. Melody happily beckoned her in and placed her on a love seat so she could watch her speed through the purchase options on her browser, moving her fingers like a skater – there was an elegance to it, how she skated from one piece of clothing to another, moving from a coat to the right accessories to match with it – split-toe shoes in degradé sequins and long turquoise gloves. Melody put a 'heart' by each and as she did, she felt if not more loved then more grounded. The faster her fingers moved, the more she tapped, the more earthed she felt. She'd been so panicked when she'd opened her laptop, but now she could breathe.

'And you don't even have to actually buy any of it!' laughed Gail. 'It looks so satisfying just to put it in the virtual basket.'

'Of course we buy it!' snapped Melody.

'But . . .'

'It's all research for my own work.'

'I don't think that's how . . .' Gail trailed off.

'Yes. Ezra's business manager marks any clothes I buy as expenses.'

And she hit 'purchase', her credit card details already encrypted within the site so it only took two taps.

'They bring it same day. Because I spend enough.'

Ezra knocked on her door, though it was open. 'Oh, hello, Gail.'

'Hi,' she said nonchalantly. 'Agata fell asleep so I . . .' but she didn't have to explain as his attention had moved to his wife.

'Darling! I have great news. The best nose in the world has agreed to create your scent. He's practically a recluse, he only takes one commission a year.'

'He's in Paris?'

'In Amsterdam.'

'Oh,' Melody replied, like a deflating balloon, Amsterdam never having been a point on her psychic dream map as a little girl in Poland.

'No, honey, it's good! That's where the fragrance foundation was launched. My people talked to him and he's going to work with me.'

'You mean with *me*.'

'With you, of course. Are you excited?'

Using all her strength, she gathered her joy and leapt into his arms. He carried her around the room as Gail averted her eyes.

Dar had been texting her for a few hours to come home and she'd been ignoring her, too. The messages were escalating in stress, but because they were flat words on a screen, Gail was able to dismiss her part in it, even though she said she'd be back hours ago, and her mother's anxiety was, in this instance, her fault. She had taken the right dose at the right time and wasn't going to end up in a police car again.

Satisfied he'd pleased his wife, Ezra retired to his office. Agata kept sleeping and just before midnight the order arrived, delivered by a young man wearing an immaculate suit and a sad face. Melody laid everything down on the floor of her bedroom. Arranged this way, it looked like the macabre act of a serial killer, humans felled, dressed up and posed. Then, to Gail's horror, she got up and went to her perfume shelf. And retrieved one by one the right scent for the right outfit, and sprayed each one of them.

'You won't be able to return them now though.'

'That's the point,' Melody answered intently. 'I'm holding myself to account. I must keep them and make them work for me.'

Then she looked at Gail.

'I actually thought this one might suit you.'

She unzipped a garment bag to reveal a pair of skin-tight, calf-length pedal pushers, zipped at the hip, like something a bad girl in a fifties melodrama would wear. Gail wondered if Melody had given them to her because she thought she was bad or because she wanted her to be.

'Put them on.'

Gail put them on in the bathroom with the door ajar so Melody could watch. She heard footsteps on the stairs beyond the room. The footsteps paused and Gail paused mid zip. In the bathroom mirror she saw, reflected in the hallway, Ezra see her. He pretended that he hadn't and kept ascending. 'I think I'm too curvy for them,' she called, to get him to turn back and keep looking, or, if he couldn't keep looking, to get him to think more about her body. Melody waded through the energy Gail was attempting to send his way, reaching out and closing the zip, saying, as she touched her:

'I'll get you something from my own line for the fund-raiser he's holding at the National Portrait Gallery.'

Her eyes widened.

'The scene of my mother's crime. Well, almost. How funny. Am I really invited?'

'The who's who of anyone who's anyone will be there. You didn't think you wouldn't be there too? You may have been there with your mother as a schoolgirl but you go back there as our guest and see what happens.'

The small dinner the Levys threw for Gail's seventeenth felt like a practice run for the gala, her own birthday paling in comparison to the party invite. She'd lied and told them her mother was busy on her birthday with work and she'd be on her own. They said they couldn't possibly let her be by herself for her birthday and Melody quickly made a reservation. Gail had been excited for it to be just the four of them and didn't feel bad about excluding her mum, with whom she'd had a snuggle in bed that morning.

She was wearing the pedal pushers Melody had bought her, which she'd paired with a pair of heeled mules she'd found on an expedition to the back of Dar's cramped closet. She wore ballet flats for the bus there, then slipped her heels on when she knew she was on the right street. A passing drunk man offered her his arm to steady herself as she made the change, laughing good-naturedly when she rejected him.

It only took a few steps to catch the rhythm of the bad-girl outfit, and she swayed her hips from side to side as she pushed open the glass door.

Her heart sank when she entered the restaurant and found Terry Loft sitting at the table. He was leaning next to Melody as if she were actually his mother, but still taking peeks down her top when he could get away with it. Rather than upbraiding Terry for this, Ezra laughed. 'He's only human!'

Agata was leaning as far away from Terry as she could.

It was an upmarket tapas restaurant with lots of small plates. Gail supposed the smallness of the servings was why they were here, in order to give Agata a chance to take or leave things without feeling too much pressure. Restaurants were their own minefield.

Gail's phone kept pinging and pinging as each dish was brought to the table. She kicked off her mother's heels under the table.

'You got a boyfriend you been keeping from us?' Terry smiled.

'No!' she said, sounding angrier than she'd meant to.

'OK, OK, keep your hair on,' said Ezra.

'I was only being funny!' Terry beamed. His teeth were the gleaming white mints you eat at the end of a cheap Chinese meal.

Ezra patted the boy's arm.

'Hey, hey. Everyone here is here because they're family.'

She cringed when Ezra said these stupid things, each pat phrase ladled with the accent he'd grown up with, the overwhelming flavour brought to the forefront. Nobody can actually smell what they smell of and nobody can hear their own accent.

Ezra said ugly and clumsy things while clad in the finest, most elegant garments, and this was where she began to feel confused. She wanted very much to have his attention, even if he was making fun of her, but if he *was* making fun of her she didn't want it to be in front of other people, especially not a fool like Terry Loft. What footballer even gets called 'Terry' nowadays?

In these moments, she felt how she had on buses when her mother had asked, 'Do you want your gloves?' and even though there was nothing inherently wrong with a mother asking her daughter if she needed her gloves, Gail had been so mortified she'd had to turn her head and pretend she could not hear.

Gail was always turning her back to Dar, moving her shoulders protectively against her questioning. On the times she'd been made to accompany her, she'd hated how small Dar's signs were at rallies, worse than if they'd been big and bright. People had to come close to read what they said as there were always too many words – she could not make any of her protest points concisely. Shame of her mother and now shame at Ezra hit different parts of her. Ezra, she felt instinctively, there was no blocking – you could only be louder and sharper than him.

'Happy birthday.' Ezra pushed a gift towards her.

'Thank you.'

'Have a look first. Go on. Look!'

Opening a long purple box, she pulled out a Cartier Ballon Bleu mechanical watch.

'It's rose gold without diamonds,' said Melody.

'Yeah but tell her,' said Terry, anxiously '. . . the one with diamonds costs *less* than the one without diamonds. I know all about watches. This one's twenty-five grand, the one with diamonds only twenty-two.'

'Terry,' Ezra patted the boy's shoulder. 'You don't have to tell her that.'

'Why?' He looked wounded.

'Well, son, it's a bit vulgar.'

'I just wanted her to know what you done for her. That she'd understand her value.'

'I chose it because it was the prettiest.' Melody smiled. 'Thank you so much.'

'I helped!' said Agata. 'We told you Dad does the best gifts.'

'And I thought it would look good with the dress Melody's sending you for the gala,' Ezra said.

Agata added, 'It would even look good in a mental hospital, if you ever end up back there.' The two girls collapsed into giggles.

Whenever Terry felt left behind, he forged ahead: 'What do you mean she's mental?'

'I used to be,' said Gail, quietly, looking at the other diners. 'I had a moment. I'm not any more.'

'She's actually a *great* influence on me,' cooed Agata. It was flirty. Gail picked up on that. Terry didn't, assuming like all men his age, and certainly all footballers, that any flirting was for him.

When she got home and told her about Agata's joke, Dar was disgusted, or professed to be.

'That's your private medical information. Do they think this is funny?'

It hadn't been funny for Dar, those nights watching her daughter in the hospital. She'd have something in common, something to actually discuss, with Ezra if they'd ever one day meet.

The clock closing on midnight, Gail kept touching the watch on her wrist as she wrote.

Dear George,
You're the only one I could say this to without you flipping out. I know I can say it to you because I

know how it feels to go downhill. It feels amazing. You feel unstoppable. Much, much freer and more confident than when you weren't speeding out of control. I don't begrudge you anything. If you can't get it right, I guess what I'm saying is: maybe we can be out of control together.

Love

Gail

Then she sealed the letter and took off the watch, knowing to put it away and never, ever let her mother see it.

CHAPTER 23

A week before the gala, there was much excitement in the Levy house: a girl-group member striking out with her first solo single was wearing a Melody gown in the promotional poster. The papers all covered the pop star's evolution from bubblegum to refined, Melody's dress the approved-of end result. Ezra had to admit, the fabric was the best of the best – Melody had an eye. It had come from an Irish silk factory she'd found on a late-night internet deep dive when she was high and had the spendies. He requested, once the photos hit the papers, that the factory become exclusive to him, or rather, to Melody. The dress was high necked and gothic, hand sewn by the old ladies. Ezra had not understood it, nor liked it, but the old ladies had done a superb job.

It didn't matter to Ezra that he had paid to place it on the pop star, who had yet to see the money from her new record deal – in fact, he preferred it that way. It was safer. It's how his father had been. Ezra didn't mind continuing this brand of 'business acumen', wearing it with pride. Just not enough pride to tell Melody what he'd done. He had, in fact, further paid people to stop her from finding out.

With this first win, it wouldn't be hard to place her clothes on A-listers at the fundraiser. Who would dare to attend his gala without kowtowing to the charity cause closest to his heart: Melody's happiness?

He'd even pulled strings and arranged a photo shoot for September *Vogue* – Melody so tall and willowy, arm in arm with the old ladies, them used as comic foil but still, it made them all look good, the eco upcycling and all. He hoped Parkers would see it and grasp how badly they'd fucked up.

Though events where she'd potentially be seen had previously caused Agata great stress, she seemed excited about this one and the mischief she and Gail could get up to. The idea of surreptitious champagne in a museum after hours was intoxicating to anyone, no matter their mental state. Agata had asked if Gail could come to the gala and Melody had said 'Of course' before Ezra could even answer. He was going to say yes, but he didn't love having the words taken out of his mouth.

Another thing that happened the week before the event: he almost blew it with his delicate daughter and her eating. So miraculous was her recovery, the family tried not to watch Agata when she occasionally consumed things in front of them. It was like trying not to stare at a cat that walks into the room during a dinner party. The small portions, the time she'd asked for a little bit more, *please*. It was like living in a dream.

It had been an afternoon when the girls were planning their return to school for the autumn term, and he had happened to wander down to the TV room from his office. He saw Gail's attention flick over to him, he wasn't blind to that, and, as a redirect, he stopped Agata as she was dipping a rich tea biscuit into her coffee. 'Wait, don't eat that biscuit,' he said, as her hand hovered above the mug. She assumed, of course, it was because she had gone beyond recovery and was now getting fat. Though he tried, he couldn't explain that he'd stopped her due to an aversion of cross species, the tea biscuit in coffee, that it turned his stomach like using the Abbey Road crossing by mistake.

His words were spindly against his heavy presence, feeling instantly like lies, even to him, who knew them to be true. And that's when Gail stepped in, trying to make light of his contortions.

'He's only saying he doesn't approve of your inter-racial snack, he's been influenced by the right wing press he owns.'

It relieved the tension, slightly. He was grateful. Melody was impressed by how Gail had herded him. She didn't see it as flirtation because she knew Gail would never be his type. And didn't see that Ezra's original comment to Agata had been, in its way, a version of flirtation. That this was something fathers tried with teenage daughters. That he had been so intently focused on her body because he didn't want her to dismantle it and die. But that if she hadn't pursued this decimation of the self, he might have, like other fathers, been noticing her body develop and, like other fathers, not been sure where to put that noticing. That maybe Agata had done everything she did in the first place so as not to make him uncomfortable. Because terror of your child's death at least isn't social awkwardness.

The flirtation was the point of the joke and Gail ran with it, taking the biscuit from Agata's hand, wrapping it in a tissue and handing it to him.

'Ha!' he said. 'Nice one!' He made a vaudeville show of tucking the soggy biscuit into the inner pocket of his blazer, which was obviously pricey, and obviously disposable to him. He checked his daughter was OK, then, having done so, checked that Gail was also OK. Because, he realised, to his confusion, that her contentment was also something he had begun hoping for.

Gail looked up at him, holding her cup of coffee. 'You lot are really closer to being Italians than you are to us Sephardim,' she teased. He noticed not for the first time that she had really pretty eyes.

He went back to his office, shaken by all this. After sitting at his desk a long while, he removed the soggy biscuit from his pocket and the soiled jacket from his body. He remembered who he was, where he'd come from, and duly went through his phone to see if there was anyone who deserved to be obliterated. Not in the way of old. Not really. But it would be soothing to know if there were anyone who it could be reasonably argued deserved to be damaged in some unspecified manner. If only he knew someone who deserved to be killed.

'We're going out now,' said Agata, pulling on a jacket of lightweight denim. The arrival of autumn was pleasant this year and she didn't need such heavy fabrics now her body fat had begun to return.

'OK, have fun, girls,' Ezra said, his arm around Melody. He was subconsciously measuring his wife, following too many recent disconnects.

The light was dimming but the air was still warm, the first day of the autumn term tomorrow seemingly a world away. The girls talked about how weird it was to be going into their final year. They didn't say how scared they both were. And Gail never let on how nervous she was to take Agata to her flat for the very first time. She covered it by slipping her arm through Agata's. She felt herself adopt the pose she'd seen Ezra take with Melody when he walked her up the street.

Once they were there, Gail made sure that her mum was still at the hospital. Dar had left the flat in its best state, with soft lamplight caressing the corniced ceiling. There were even fresh flowers on the table.

Agata had kicked off her shoes at the entrance, not out of politeness, but from the privilege of knowing someone would arrange them neatly for her.

They went into Gail's bedroom, where the lack of floor space meant they both needed to lie on the bed. She played Agata the Leonard Cohen album that had just come out, which he'd written knowing that he was dying. They lay over the covers, listening to 'You Want It Darker' in pin-drop silence. When it was finished Agata took a moment to speak.

'What does he mean when he says "Hineni"?'

Gail stared at the ceiling.

'It means "Here I am".'

Agata's eyes grew misty. 'It's beautiful.' No more words. Gail wondered what could be held in the silence. It was like not picking up a basket at the supermarket, carrying things with your hands until it becomes precarious, needing to choose immediately whether to become self-censoring or bold. *Bold*. Are you OK with dropping breakable things in front of strangers in the pursuit of more?

She leaned over and kissed Agata. She mimicked how she'd seen Ezra kiss Melody. At first Agata shrank back, then, after a beat, leaned into it. As their tongues intertwined, both Gail's mouth and her underwear turned from cottony to wet. Gail felt the blood pool in her clitoris and knew, just knew, that it was not something she'd be able to keep there, that it would soon leave her, the pooled blood and the feeling, too. In that moment, she felt like Clark Kent twirling into Superman inside the phone booth. As the image entered her head, she pressed Agata against the bedroom wall as if they were making out in an eighties phone booth.

'It's just for practice,' she told the still-vulnerable girl when she pulled away. She reached out and smoothed Agata's hair, as she imagined a soothing alpha male might.

'I understand,' Agata whispered.

Things were different on the first day of autumn term. Not broken, but no longer entirely safe terrain. Rather than the kiss bringing them closer, Gail could see Agata talking in the corridor and playground to girls she'd not ever made conversation with before. She saw her, too, looking away from the lessons where before she had been laser focused. Her hunger had sharpened her mind and now she wasn't starving, Agata looked around rooms to see what else was happening.

It was true, when Gail examined it, alone at lunch that first day back, that she had, after kissing Agata, very much wanted her to leave – her bed, her flat, her street. The act of closeness had made some part of her body fire up with the fear that she might have to be fused with Agata. So, yes, she'd said, 'Shouldn't you be getting home?' when she knew Agata was expecting to stay the night. She had made her leave, really. She'd wanted, too, to be left alone with thoughts of Ezra.

She hadn't pushed her out the door and up the hall and to the lift. Or had she? Had she watched her get forlornly into the waiting limo, before it pulled away past the Heath? If she had, she'd not intended it to cause a schism.

'I'm still invited to the gala, right?'

'Yes,' said Agata, 'of course – why would you even ask that?'

But they both knew it was a fair question.

She saw now that all kisses, no matter how good they might be, were a bill you could either afford or not afford to pay in the long run.

CHAPTER 24

The morning of the gala, a messenger arrived at Gail and Dar's flat by bike with a garment bag. Inside were two dresses. Dar had her judgement ready and loaded.

'How kind of Melody to send you a choice.'

Gail read the attached card.

'No, look. She says one is for me and the other is a gift for you.'

Now she lowered her weapon. 'For me? Why? Am I . . .'

'What?'

'Am I invited?' Her voice was tremulous.

'No,' said Gail, 'it's just out of kindness, I guess.'

'Good,' said Dar, reaching in and untucking the label on the second gown, 'I would never have gone.' She read the label as if parsing a legal contract.

'What are you doing?'

'Checking they're not made in a sweatshop.'

'They're couture, Mum, hand sewn in the East End of London.'

'East End couture,' Dar scoffed.

'Do you want it or not?' Gail was secretly nervous about returning to the gallery, where they'd run riot in the halls as a schoolgirl pack and now, only months later, she was expected to pass as a grown-up.

'How do you know that one's for me, Gail?'

'Because it looks older.' (Her anxiety dialled her teen angst up to cruel.)

'No. I can't accept it. I can't take his money.'

'OK, fine, I'll give it back.'

Dar put up her hand. 'No, I don't want to be rude.'

'OK. So try it on. I want to see you in it.'

'Another time. I'm so tired. You try yours on.'

Gail held it against her chest.

'It's a great colour for your eyes, honey.'

Gail stepped into the bathroom to get changed.

Dar kept talking as Gail zipped herself in: 'You have to wonder: what does he want from us in return?'

'Mum, it's from her, not him.'

'But she married him. That's worse. At least he can't help who he is.'

Gail stepped out of the bathroom and Dar gasped.

'You look *so* beautiful.'

'It does look good, I admit it.'

Gail's shoulders looked broad and powerful, her waist small, the line of the gown arcing back out over the thickness of her thighs and ass. She looked like an R. Crumb drawing sheathed in stretch jersey. It was an X shape, as in 'X marks the spot'. How could Agata stand next to her without wanting to get well? Dar truly thought her daughter was so stunning it could cure other girls' mental disorders.

They found that the right heel had also been included with the delivery, a copper metallic that gave her height but let her walk.

'Ha!' said Dar, even as she admired her. 'Copper!'
'What?'
'His *copper money* started his whole evil empire.'
'Oh. Right.'

After Gail was gone, Dar got ready to leave for her shift. But first . . .

She tried on her dress (only out of interest). It covered her completely from neck to ankle, outlining her body like a crime scene. The boning constructed inside by the East End old ladies was immaculate and everything went in and out in all the right places. The arms were so slinky, she had to stroke herself.

She sipped from a sneaky glass of red wine and looked at herself in the full-length mirror. The delicate smattering of crystals around the edges caught the light, creating the optical illusion of an aura photo.

But when on earth would she ever wear a dress like this?

She thought about sending her ex a photo. To make the school-trip incident come undone. A photo that would erase that awful day. She finished the glass of wine, then set up all the good lighting and diffused it with a scarf over a lamp. She lifted the dress and slipped off her knickers so there were no visible lines. Then she got on her knees and held the hem of her dress in her teeth, revealing her lack of underwear as the camera clicked.

After admiring the result, she deleted it all.

CHAPTER 25

The National Portrait Gallery was glowing with lights, the assigned press jostling for spots outside it. A privileged few were permitted to stand inside and snap as the VIPs entered. There were also the paparazzi who, being unassigned, followed guests up the side alleys on their entry and exit. The sight of this reminded Gail of friendships she had been in.

On seeing Gail in her stunning gown, photographers lifted their cameras quizzically like a half-erection, then dropped them again without snapping. What becomes of a girl viewed through a lens but not captured? She felt an intimidating energy coming off the museum's magnificent architecture that she'd not been aware of when they'd all been running riot on the school trip. Maybe they'd been too loud that day to notice. Or maybe the building just felt different this late, when the exhibitions should have been put to sleep for the night, lights dimmed and security half awake.

Gail got to the front of the bag check just in time to watch the Levys walk the carpet together. Agata, near the very top of the carpet, spotted Gail and motioned for her to come over and join them. She hung back, not wanting to be in the shot. Agata would get away with these pictures – the papers would say she looked great and she *would* look great: because the camera puts on ten pounds she'd look like the models they'd clipped out from magazines that first day in her bedroom.

Agata had gained just enough weight for the planes of her face to rise enough to apply makeup to. When she'd first arrived at St Saviour's, the skin was too sunken for the colours to show, her eyes were in shadow. The rosy glow on the cheeks was only obscene if you knew what she had done to herself these past years. Gail didn't know enough about the world to recognise that this look – a terribly thin teenage girl trying her best – would appeal to a certain kind of awful man. Agata tottered a moment in her heels and, falling for what should have been just a moment from Gail's sight, was lost from view.

Unsure of what to do, feeling a little lost without her, Gail pushed herself through the crowds to the main event, which was in the same gallery where Agata had stood up out of her chair and walked the day of the school trip. Ezra's plaque on the wall was the centrepiece around which all the trays of cocktails spun, his name in lights.

Once inside, Ezra was surrounded by other men who looked like him, but less handsome. They appraised Gail briefly as she approached but nothing was said. Ezra nodded, politely, as if he were not the one who'd brought her here.

'Ezra? Where did Agata get to? She was right down there at the entrance – she waved at me – but I've lost track of her.'

She wasn't sure if Agata was deliberately avoiding her following their kiss. She suspected that she was.

'Really? You've lost her?' scoffed Ezra, only half listening. 'She doesn't move that fast.'

Approaching, resplendent in royal red velvet, Melody air-kissed her, all long neck, long hair, long nails and long lashes. Gail thought it was kind of labouring the point. She looked at the ground as Ezra kissed Melody's exposed shoulder. To see her shoulder gently and surreptitiously kissed felt more intimate than if he'd bent her backwards and French kissed her. The throng of men who had had no interest in Gail all laughed with Melody's every coy pronouncement, a moving cloud that carried her off to the champagne bar.

Ezra and Gail were alone again. He nodded at her dress. 'You look smart.'

'I look *smart*?'

'It's a compliment.'

'Thank you, I guess.'

She knew she looked sexy but understood that he could never say it.

'The watch looks good.'

'Thank you,' she replied, shimmying the Cartier at him. She'd had to sneak it out in her clutch and put it on once she got there, so Dar wouldn't discover it.

'The exhibition is beautiful,' she continued, the din of the glamorous guests far, far louder than the noise they'd made when they'd visited as a class. 'Ever get sick of seeing your name in lights?'

He made a face, somewhere between Bond and a Bond villain.

'It's not in lights, it's engraved with light trained on it.'

'In marble?'

'I think so. I'm not gonna start stroking my own name to find out. Not in front of these cunts.'

'How do you know they're cunts?' she asked, remembering to engage her core to make the best line in the jersey. That was a benefit of being in school uniform: you could slouch without anyone seeing.

'Because,' he said, laughing, 'they have enough money to be here.'

He nudged her. She thought it was awful to be nudged in an evening gown.

'They never suffered and struggled like our families did.'

She nodded in agreement, still looking for Agata. Though she hoped to spot her in the crowd, she also hoped she'd stay lost a little longer. These moments with Ezra were precious, even when he said or did the wrong thing.

'Hey. I've been meaning to ask you, Ezra. Where do they come from, originally, your people?'

'Russia, way back.'

'Whereabouts?' she prodded.

'Ekaterinburg,' he answered immediately.

She went quiet.

'What?' he asked.

'Well, that would be very unusual for a Jewish family. Are you sure? You're not just thinking of the name Ekaterinburg because . . .'

'Because what?' He shrugged.

'Maybe it's a place in your brain because it's where the Romanovs were murdered by the Bolsheviks?'

He blushed deeply, knowing the moment she'd said it that she was right. Drunk on embarrassment, he took her hand, the watch sliding down her wrist. He briefly examined her fingers, with their chipped polish, letting go before anyone saw him.

'Nail polish was a big deal for my mother,' he said, having willed away the red from his cheeks. 'When I started paying for the weekly manicure for her, she knew that I had made it. She cared so much about her nails, these half-moons on them.'

She didn't know what to say, so whispered: 'You know, Natalie Wood's real name was Natasha.'

He was smiling, silent.

'You probably knew that, right?'

The embarrassment that had suffused his skin a distant memory, he raised his eyes to Gail like a very lazy lion who might one day kill her but only if he could sleep a long time first.

'I didn't know. And I don't care.'

After he was pulled away by press, she still couldn't find Agata and had no one to talk to. She walked once through the exhibition, downing two glasses of champagne and dreaming into the satin and embroidery all around her. Everywhere she looked, all these young women with older men, even in the paintings.

She drank another glass proffered her way by a temp waiter too underpaid to see she was a kid. Then, in the far corner of the room, standing beneath Sir Winston Churchill, she saw Terry Loft. His team had continued to progress to the final round because of the way he'd carried their dedicated enthusiasm with his precise gift, and he was surrounded by girls. From the centre of them, his lilting accent rose into the air like a lit amaretto wrapper. He saw Gail and pulled away from them and towards her.

CHAPTER 26

Dear George,

My whole body is shaking as I write this to you. You are the only one I can confide in. I don't know where to start. I don't . . .

Terry said to me, 'You look like something in full bloom.' That's the first thing to mention. That when he saw me in my dress, he didn't say something vulgar or stupid like he usually does. He said something that moved me.

We snuck away from everyone else. He shook the girls off like a dog shaking away water. The way a dog enjoys that? You could see he enjoyed getting rid of them.

He said he'd take me to find her. Then he had taken my hand in his and we'd wandered the halls and because it was so special to be there out of hours it was special or at least interesting to be with him after hours, too. On a few glasses of champagne, or the ambience of the room, his accent sounded really beautiful — I admit it made me reassess him, like he could live up to the portraits on the walls.

He kicked a Fanta can all the way up the hall, past the faces looking down on us from centuries past. He dribbled it this way and that as if I were the right audience for football. And I must have been the right audience because when he was done, I clapped. I heard myself do it! He bowed to me, like one of the courtiers in the Tudor wing.

Eventually we kind of gave up on finding Agata and were in some kind of a side room, a hall that didn't really have a purpose except linking one exhibition to another. Only no one was there because it had nothing but death masks and the sculpture of a man's head drawn from his own blood, held in the centre of a refrigerated display. Terry asked me to finish the joint with him, blowing the smoke into my mouth with his. It must have interacted with my medicine or the alcohol or both, because it hit me fast.

I could feel myself getting hazy and ready to be kissed, running my fingers along his arms. Ezra was his father figure too. He wasn't boring or uncouth and vulgar, a trashy soccer player any more. We could be beautiful together. He kissed me and I kissed him back, deeply. George! It was like when you spotted the love of your life in an audience of sixty thousand people as you sang on stage in Brazil. That's how it felt.

He touched me very gently on my lips. I touched his. I had been the one to kiss the girls, to make the move on Faith and then Agata. But he was the one who kissed me and it felt good to be chosen. He was so beautiful, right there by the death masks. I touched his hat hair and it wasn't so silly when your fingers were in it. When you're high and you're touching it, his hair was actually lovely. Then, he put one hand on the front of my neck, which I wasn't expecting. That wasn't how it had been in my mind when I pictured men and women kissing. He rested it there but I didn't like it but I didn't know if it was OK not to like it and just as I was thinking that he said:

'You like that.'

Have you ever done anything you didn't want to do, George? Out on the Heath?

So then, because it wasn't how it would be in my mind, and because the head made of blood was freaking me out, I wanted to stop. And he didn't want to stop. That was the problem. Faith and Agata – I'd been in charge of them. And now I wasn't in charge.

When I said 'no' it was like letting a vampire know that you know they're a vampire. Then they have to kill you. His whole physicality changed. All the power from the pitch filled his body.

I tried to leave and he tried to block my path. I tried hard not to show I was afraid. I tried to flatter and cajole my way back out of this purposeless chamber and into the room with the rest of the guests.

'Put it in your mouth,' he said.

'What?'

'Come on, enough games.'

But it wasn't enough games and I didn't have enough mouth and that's when he really pressed his hand on my throat.

When he gave me a moment to breathe, I called out for my mother.

That made him laugh and his laughter gave me a split second to get out.

I haven't told anyone but you and Ezra.

But, please, don't worry about me. Don't ever worry about me.

As always, let me know if I can help you at all.

Love
Gail

CHAPTER 27

When she got away back into the crowds, Terry Loft simply gathered his things like nothing had happened and left for the night with two of the women he'd been talking to before. Gail looked around the gallery. The party was beginning to wind down, but Ezra was still there. The cameras were now packed up and gone. He saw the state of Gail, how her makeup was smeared and how hard she shook and, guiding her through a back exit, nudged her into his limo, getting in quickly behind her.

'Drive,' he barked.

The chauffeur took off at speed.

He pressed a button and his chauffeur was shut out.

'Where's Melody?' she finally asked.

'She's gone home with Agata. What happened to you?'

She was crying so hard as she told him and his eyes flashed all black, the whole iris seemed to become pupil.

'I'm sorry for coming to you. I didn't know where to go.'

'My driver will take you home.'

'You believe me?'

'Yes,' he said, 'I believe you.'

'This is just between us?'
'Yes.' He wouldn't look at her. 'Of course.'

Her mother was asleep on the sofa when Gail woke up the next day. She went in to school, wondering if anyone could see what had happened, what had almost happened . . . what *had* happened? But nobody seemed to notice anything, only that she was late and that Agata wasn't in at all. She'd had a whole glass of champagne so was taking the day off school with a hangover.

Gail studied her face in the bathroom mirror. How many girls had he done this to? Would he do it to Agata? Had he already tried? She tried to figure out her options. Whether to go to the police or to deal with it herself. She tried to imagine a scenario where she involved her mother.

Waking in the night as her body tried to break down too many champagne cocktails, Melody found that Ezra was not beside her. She padded out of bed, knowing that if he were sleeping off a hangover, he'd do it in a different bedroom. She knew when he finally rose he'd want a bacon sandwich ('And don't tell my mum'). Herself, she found the best way to recover from too much alcohol was exercise.

She went down to the swimming pool before dawn had even broken. There was no point in putting on a swimsuit, so she just tugged off her nightie. If there had been anybody else there, they might have been distracted by the sight of her naked body before noticing the more pressing figure in the room.

It was like a spotlight was on him. The stars sliced out of the ceiling had a full moon above them and they studded his body with their glow. Melody screamed until her throat felt shredded, but it took a while for security to hear as the dome of the swimming pool ceiling muffled sound.

By the time Gail left school for home, the *Evening Standard* had it on their cover: Terry Loft had been found face-down in the pool of Ezra Levy's home. The golden boy who'd taken his team to the very top had been staying with him as a guest following Ezra's charity gala the night before.

Terry had been taken to hospital where he now lay in a coma, his mother on her way from Ireland to be at his side.

Dar was sitting up at the window with its perfect view when Gail arrived back from school. It was open, letting in a chill. Unusually, Dar was smoking.

'What is it, Mum?'

Dar stubbed out the cigarette and clung to her when she walked in.

'Have you seen the news about the footballer? Did you cross paths with him ever?'

'Yeah, I met him.'

'It's so awful. I'm sorry, darling, my heart is racing.' She closed the window. 'He's in our hospital.'

'Fuck.'

Did Dar know what had happened to her? What had almost happened? Could she tell and was just prodding?

'The papers are all over it. My floor was crawling with journalists.'

'Well, it's a horrible thing to happen, but it would have just been too much champagne. Everyone knew he was a partier.'

Dar nodded, whispering: 'They said he was like a son to Ezra. I almost feel sorry for him.'

Gail tried to get information out of Agata when she returned to school, but she still seemed unbalanced by the alcohol she'd drunk, going so far as to eat a chocolate bar in one sitting rather than spreading it out over the course of a whole day.

Ezra was inscrutable when she stopped by with Agata after school, security pushing a camera crew out of the way to clear the path for them. Melody was at the kitchen table, drawing a design for her perfume bottle, ahead of even knowing what the scent was.

'It's horrible about Terry,' Gail said. 'I'm so sorry.'

Melody spoke in tranquil tones suggesting a tranquiliser rather than inner peace. 'Thank you, dear. What are you doing in half-term? I'm going to Amsterdam to meet up with the nose who's making my perfume. I'm taking Agata and Ezra suggested we travel by Eurostar to make it more scenic. Why don't you come with us?'

Was she really not going to talk about the cameras outside and the drowning in her pool? *Was* this just a tranquiliser or was she silent by decree?

'Is Ezra going?'

'He has work, all this stuff with Terry. So unpleasant.'

Ezra walked in and, as stressed as he was, even though she was the one who'd brought this new trouble on him, when he saw Gail at the table he was pleased. He had someone to cook his meals, to drive him, to pack his suitcase when he travelled. He really didn't know what Gail was *for* and that meant he kept coming back around to her.

Agata was having a vitamin drip. When Melody left the room to sign for a Net a Porter delivery, Gail quickly got closer to him and asked, 'Did you do that for me?'

'Do what?' He had on his chirpy East End voice. You could never get past it. It was like a set of veneers, made for TV, and when he was desperate it expanded beyond being teeth caps, morphed and became a mask.

'If you did do it, thank you.'

'Stop it,' he said, stern.

'I'm sorry,' she whispered.

'Things unfold the way they unfold. I don't like bad men. I don't take well to things getting done to girls and women. That's all I have to say. Go with them on their little half-term jaunt. It will be good for you. I've got everything covered here.'

She didn't like the idea of being there without him, it felt strange. But his money was an extension of Ezra and that was second best – if there were no other option involving him, she'd take it.

Agata seemed to have been rattled enough by Terry's accident to take a step towards their friendship. As she had made clear in the weeks following their kiss, she was not sure it was right for her. But now, with the unease of what had happened to the boy, she felt afraid of what else might be out there. So when Gail asked if she wanted her there in Amsterdam, she insisted that she did.

Gail pitched it to her mother that night.

'Melody is going to Amsterdam to meet the nose who's making her perfume. It will just be three nights. I'd like to take them up on their very kind offer.'

'It's not for you to say it's a very kind offer,' sniffed Dar. 'Why are you narrating it while you ask me? That's weird. Why are you holding so close to them when all this awful stuff has just happened? I think you should be staying away from them.'

'But you've said that from the start.'

'Well, now I really mean it!'

Gail felt her way into her most persuasive voice. 'I'm freaked out by it all and you'll be working. I don't want to be alone in the flat at the moment.'

Dar sighed and put her arm around her.

'It's all very upsetting.'

Gail, leaning into her, changed tack when she should have stayed the course. 'And he's arranged to have the Anne Frank House open early just for us.'

Dar straightened.

'Why are they opening early for him? That's disgusting. They're a charity.'

'I guess because he gives millions of pounds each year to Jewish causes.'

'Ridiculous! He gets to examine genocide out of hours because he's so rich?'

'Mum, please,' she came closer, leaned her head on her. 'Please? Do I get to go?' And then she added, 'You smell nice today, Mum.'

Dar agreed to let her go and Gail set about packing.

The papers, having photographed Terry Loft's weeping mother, didn't at first try to unpick how exactly he'd ended up in Ezra Levy's swimming pool all alone so late at night – that was just something glamorous figures had done since time immemorial. They did wonder whether, at any point, there had been anyone else there with him. CCTV, which Ezra Levy was a notorious stickler for after a robbery a few years back, had for some reason not been working.

It was a tragedy. Obviously, it was a terrible tragedy. But beyond the tragedy of it, the uncomfortable fact remained: without Terry, his winning team did not get to win. The feeling was they might power through and clinch the championship cup *in his honour*. It would have been the perfect end to a rousing sports movie. But Ezra wasn't much for movies. It was hard enough for him to sit still in the stands where all eyes were on him, let alone in a darkened room where no one would notice him leave.

'We wanted to do it for his mum,' said one of Terry's closest team mates, before dissolving into sobs and turning away from the camera.

Right after it happened, before the final took place, all the fans on the street had offered condolences when they saw Ezra. But that turned once they'd lost. Ezra was in their memes and on their placards. The darkest corners of the internet ran rumours and accusations that expanded like ink into more mainstream sites. It was his swimming pool. It was his fault. Click here to research *his past that the papers can't talk about.*

The tabloids waited outside his home another day, until, eventually, Ezra was suddenly joining them on their half-term trip to Amsterdam.

PART 5

CHAPTER 28

Ezra had arrived in Amsterdam on edge, head down in a city where all the local men were friendly, tall and relaxed. They smiled when they passed him in a way that set his radar off.

'Hi! Good afternoon!' Melody, easily influenced by her surroundings, said to small dogs or commuters carrying bunches of tulips in their arms. He thought it was absurd for the Dutch to walk around carrying tulips, like if he walked around dressed as Tevye and singing 'If I Were a Rich Man'. Melody ambled through the cobbled streets as if in her own musical montage, as if what had happened in their swimming pool had been a mere misunderstanding long since cleared up.

Gail could see it made Ezra uncomfortable, the people of Amsterdam and their ease in the world. Cajoled by Melody, trying to 'act normal' as his lawyer had instructed, he accompanied them to the Van Gogh Museum. He who owned a football club and its accompanying stadium seemed infuriated that other people existed, let alone in such crowds. He was madder still at Van Gogh for letting himself get fucked up.

They all went back to the hotel, apart from Melody who departed for her big scent discussion. She returned, elated, from her meeting with the nose. She tried to initiate gratitude sex with her husband but his lawyer reported that the papers were still digging, and he wasn't in the mood to be thanked. By the time they reconvened for dinner, Ezra was visibly struggling.

Across the hall, Agata was in the deep bathtub, noticing that the places on her body that had grown excess downy hair to keep her warm in the worst of the illness were now smooth again.

At a desk by the window, Gail felt sharp flashes back to Terry Loft's hand on her throat, back to the millisecond it had felt good before it felt bad. She felt momentarily confused about which feeling had been which. She hoped growing up would mean knowing, always and with clarity, exactly which feeling belonged where and how to store them appropriately. Roll up the bad memories or fold them flat? Carry them in the cabin when you travel or check them, so you'd feel lighter but a stranger could rifle through?

Gail had decided to take a cue from behaviour she'd observed in her time spent with the Levys, and show up for this trip as if nothing bad or difficult had recently happened, but it was hard.

She squeezed her eyes shut, balled up her fists, released it all but felt no better. So she fished in her handbag and got out her pen. She needed to divert her mind even if she had little to offer this time.

Dear George,
Amsterdam is far more beautiful than any city I've
ever been to. Not sure how much you see of cities when

you tour. Maybe you only see the venue and your
room. But you should see Amsterdam. You should tour
again just to see it. Van Gogh cutting off his ear
because he felt rejected . . . now that's a man grasping
for intimacy and freedom in one fell swoop. It made
me think of you.
 Love
 Gail

Wandering the city alone, she posted it before she had a chance to add in what happened next.

Agata, having assured Gail she wanted her to be there, acted less enthused once they arrived. On noting the vanishing of her downy fur, she was beginning to restrict her food intake again, and the lack of energy was affecting her mood. She complained in the Van Gogh Museum, as if competing with the long-dead painter's pain, and then declined to accompany them on their specially arranged out-of-hours visit to the Anne Frank House.

One of the guards who searched their bags before they entered was Polish and he and Melody chatted in their own language and, even though it was brief, Ezra didn't like it. He entered the sacred space pissy and small.

But with each step, Gail watched him come back into his body. The museum was self-guided, which presented a challenge to each of them in their own way. Touchingly, Melody had arranged a special outfit for the annexe. Having been warned there were a great deal of stairs, she had on what appeared to be luxe hiking boots. The entrance to the living quarters was so narrow, they had to walk through in single file. As she ascended the first set of stairs, she turned around to Gail. She thought Melody was about to acknowledge the heaviness of the air in this place that had contained so much terror. But Melody simply smiled and coyly said, 'No peeking!'

Once inside the annexe, Melody arranged her face differently, pulling down a part of the headband she was wearing, and Gail understood it was a veil, perhaps to indicate respect.

'Oh!' Melody exclaimed, as she looked around. 'This is actually quite spacious.'

Ezra and Gail grimaced at each other.

'Wow!' Melody clapped her hands. 'The light is really beautiful up here.'

Streaming in from three different windows, it illuminated where the eight doomed souls had huddled in silent fear, awaiting the heart-dropping sound of jackboots on the pavement outside.

'And look at the view!' Melody marvelled. 'You can see all along the east canal!'

For a terrible moment, Ezra feared Melody might be about to ask if they could make an offer on the place. This was his first experience with her of partner shame and he felt it to his core.

When they reached Anne's bedroom, all Gail could think was how terrible it would be to have to share your adolescent space not even with a family member but with a middle-aged dentist who your parents had insisted on finding space for. Worse still, one who was hiding from mass murder while simultaneously battling heartbreak. That you might have to have a wall up not only around your teenage awkwardness but also his late-life romantic heartbreak. That those feelings could exist beside the genocidal terror.

In her attic, on her tiny patch of bedroom wall, were Anne's movie stars, cut out and pasted from magazines like all teenage girls do, as Gail and Agata often had, now yellowed with the passage of time.

'Look,' said Ezra, leaning in. 'That's Queen Elizabeth and Princess Margaret.'

Two toddlers that Gail had thought perhaps a music hall double act were in fact their royal highnesses in their youths, which would then expand to old age. Anne's youth would end here, beneath them. What dreams had been projected onto the royal sisters?

She thought of all the letters she'd sent George and wondered for the first time: what was the escape dream she'd been having through them? Once the Frank family and their other hidden friends made it through (and the family knew once the allies had landed in Normandy that they *would* make it), would Anne have agitated to go to England next? To Hollywood? Somewhere to pursue her icons and her dreams in person? Gail put her hand on her heart, overcome.

Melody, in her specialist shoes for viewing Holocaust Hiding Spaces, had ventured beyond them to the final floor. Ezra saw that Gail looked close to fainting and when he caught her, only the cutout movie stars saw.

'I know,' he said, 'I know.' And he held her and, instead of fainting, she kissed him. He kissed her back for a moment, Melody moving on the floor above. It wasn't really clear who started it – a referee would have to watch a replay many times and then it would still be a controversial decision. What was clear was they both needed it. They were there as long as they could be, before they pulled apart, silent, afraid of being discovered.

CHAPTER 29

They ate out on their final night, in a restaurant that had recently received its first Michelin star. Ezra entered the gilded space listening out for the soft hum of rumour. The baked-in edginess because of Terry Loft was now frosted with being on edge because of the ill-judged kiss.

It happened to be Rosh Hashanah, which also annoyed him when Gail pointed it out. This wasn't a Jewish restaurant – or even that Jewish fallback, a Chinese restaurant – so he couldn't quite see how marking it together pertained to a religious holiday of any sort. It was just a fancy restaurant. One where they knew who he was, and knew in advance that he was coming. The news of Terry's accident had of course made it here – Amsterdam was a big football town – and other diners turned to look as they sat down.

Melody seemed delighted by the eyes, swallowing everyone's gaze like they were the finest oysters. She leaned into Ezra, who put his arm around her.

The restaurant had the right lighting so they all looked good – Agata looked the healthiest she had in years; where once her skin had been sunken, now it had dewiness to it, as if she were, as she ought to be at sixteen, blooming rather than decaying. The willpower of the anorexic teen girl had shocked Ezra, the closing down of the body rearranged like a failed game of Tetris. It did not fit. *It did not fit for him.* He was so happy when she seemed to turn a corner, because he loved her, but also because life was easier again.

Until Terry.

Melody always looked beautiful, but tonight her pale peach outfit was translucent in the glow. The row of diamond earrings in each ear were like lights around a mirror. She kept smelling her wrist and sighing with pleasure.

'I'm so glad we got him for you,' Ezra said, patting her stiffly.

'You got me the best. You always get me the best.'

She sniffed herself again and moaned. At first he was pleased but it quickly became grating.

Gail. Gail looked good, if you were into that sort of thing. He knew why Terry had gone for her, the fucking idiot. She'd find, he knew, decent men who were all about her looks. He could never imagine it himself (he told himself, despite what had happened that day) but then his type was his wife (he told himself): clean, calm, cool, blonde, blue-eyed.

'To mark this trip, please everyone go round the table,' chirped Melody, who had foolishly combined Percocet with optimism, 'and say what is the smell you find most comforting.' When she was wasted you could hear that English was her second language.

They looked at each other.

'For me, as a little girl in Poland, it was my grandmother's breakfast buns. The cinnamon. And when I walked in to meet him, I smelled it instantly: he had that right there as the dry note after the top note of rose is gone. Like he somehow knew about my childhood!' (She had sent him a long email in advance of meeting, describing the smells of her childhood.)

Ezra remembered how Gail had questioned the propensity, around an anorexic, for gourmand scents.

'Um. I love the smell of fresh laundry,' said Agata. *Perfect*, he thought, ruffled at the fantasy that she was trying to get away from him – *she's chosen something inedible and something someone else has to do for her*.

It was Gail's turn.

'What scent do I find comforting?' She rapped her chipped fingernails on the table. 'To be honest . . .'

'Yes, get on with it,' said Ezra. She raised her eyes to him, warning him, *be nice*.

'. . . my own used underwear.'

The women tittered, Agata forgetting to be annoyed.

Melody pinched Gail sweetly. 'I wonder what the nose would make of you!'

'Take me to him!' Gail laughed.

'No,' said Ezra, humourless, 'he's on an exclusive eighteen-month contract to Melody.'

'Melody,' Gail asked, 'now you know exactly what it's going to smell like, have you settled on the logo?'

'I think so,' and she started to sketch her idea on the napkin, which she seemed not to care was made from fabric, not paper. She pushed it towards Gail.

'What do you think?'

It was a rose with fishes swimming around it.

'Oh. Can I be honest?'

'Of course,' she replied.

'Please don't be,' snapped Ezra. He was being nasty. He was being dangerous.

Gail flattened out the napkin. 'What are you trying to say with this? Because it might be a little bit confusing. It's a bit diffuse.'

The Percocet was flooding Melody's long limbs. 'I want you to feel submerged by this scent, like you're in your own underwater dream where you're the ruler.'

'May I?' Gail picked up the pen. She sketched a little on her own napkin as the waiter arrived at the table. They said 'Two minutes' and sent him away.

Ezra whispered something in his wife's ear. Gail, who still wasn't certain if she could imagine having actual sex with him, thought she might explode with envy. She knew she could imagine him whispering in her ear, even if she couldn't tune in to what the whispers she wanted were. Just the hot breath on her ear. She wanted his hot breath for her own, to keep and wear in a locket around her neck.

So, to make Melody feel like an outsider, Gail said the Rosh Hashanah prayer while Ezra stared her down, fuming. Melody seemed unruffled, recording her on her phone, smiling, while Agata looked at the tablecloth in a grump that had segued to misery.

Gail did not know where the words were coming from, did not know how she remembered them, but they kept coming.

Agata, of course, would not eat any of the bread on the table, then when Melody was offered some, she demurred. Then the waiter offered it to Gail and she said no, and was irritated when Ezra said, loudly:

'Really? I thought for sure you were a bread girl.'

And Gail sat up tall and said, 'It's meant to be unleavened bread. Isn't it?'

And Ezra leaned in and said, 'Wrong holiday and wrong prayer,' and he put a roll in his mouth and bit off a hunk of bread, while diners watched.

'I don't bloody know,' Gail retorted, clinging to dignity, 'my grandpa didn't even let my mum join a synagogue.'

Both the other women looked nervous, even Melody in her reverie.

'Why's that, then?'

'Because he wanted Mum to integrate. So she'd be safe.'

Talking about safety in any context raised his hackles enough that his security, on another table, took note and scanned the room, not aware it was the schoolgirl he'd stupidly kissed who was setting him off.

'Oy, I understand his point,' he said quietly.

'Then why do you always say words like *zaftig* and *oy*, like you're such a big Jew?'

'Can you please stop saying that word. You don't know who's around us.'

'These guys? The Dutch? Their people helped. Their people hid us.'

His face was turning red with anger. 'Yeah, and some of them were Jew-hunters, so shut your mouth in public.'

It was a kind of flirting. Nobody, except deep in her subconscious his daughter, registered that what Ezra and Gail were doing had an erotic undertone, as any talk of hiding often does. And Agata had starved the subconscious into submission for so long now that it was slow and creaky to action what it might reasonably share with her.

Her having no accessible subconscious was why Gail had, if she were honest with herself, come to tire of Agata so quickly. Yeah, she'd helped her get better. But ultimately there was nothing really there for her to save. She'd felt it when she kissed her.

But Ezra and Gail both knew what the bottom note was beneath their banter, and while he resented her deeply – this unprepossessing little girl – for drawing out of him a dangerous kiss, she could not have been more thrilled. She felt alive. She felt she was speeding downhill, grabbing bread rolls as she went, stuffing them into her pockets, throwing them at spectators, tearing them and using them as under-eye masks, siphoning them, back through time and space to hungry ancestors.

The waiter returned to the table.

'Smell me!' shrieked Melody.

The waiter stood there, blinking as she waved her wrist back and forth at him.

'You can smell her,' said Ezra, deflating, 'it's for research. Tell us if you'd buy this for your wife.'

'Tell us if you'd buy it for your mistress!' Melody laughed.

The waiter wafted the scent towards him with his hands, both of which were free as the restaurant was too fancy to have him write the order down.

'Lovely,' he said, nervously. 'Very lovely.'

'You see!' Melody cried.

'The bottle design will look like this.' She showed the unhappy waiter her sketch of the rose and the fishes. Then she held it up to the next table. Everyone nodded.

Ezra ordered first – a burger, well done and Gail interjected that he should have his burger medium, not well done and when he said 'No,' she said, 'Well, I think that's criminal.' Melody, in her haze, dragged her eyes up as the word 'criminal' hung in the air. Ezra laughed, not nervously but not confidently.

In contrast to her stepmother, Agata did not look up at the waiter when he asked her for her order. Finally Ezra let him go, thanking him profusely, so profusely that the waiter looked stricken with horror. Ezra smiled, revealing his too-white caps, and Gail flashed back to Terry Loft.

Maybe that's why she did what she did next. To try to wrest some control.

When the food began to arrive, Gail excused herself to the ladies' room. That's where she said she was going, but instead she walked to the front of house and, whispering that they were not to let on, handed the maitre d her credit card – her mother's credit card technically, with her name as an extension, given to her for this trip abroad in case of emergency. The host looked unsure but took the card and ran it before handing it back with a nervous expression.

When Gail returned to the table, she could see that Melody was laying her head on the table while Ezra upbraided Agata.

'When the waiter took our order you were very rude.'

'I don't think I was?' she answered tremulously.

'You wouldn't look at him.'

'I was shy.'

It was bizarre, that the focus was on her perceived misdeed and not on Melody being wasted, or Ezra having joined this trio in the first place because the internet thought he'd drowned his best footballer. Gail felt a genuine pang of affection and sadness for Agata.

'It doesn't matter if you're shy: the waiter thinks you're rude, the other diners think you're rude, it reflects on me. That's who they're taking it out on. I can't afford to have people telling stories about me, saying I am a disrespectful person because of how I've raised my kid.'

The word 'kid' stung Agata, and though she had spent two years deliberately shrinking her body so that it would stay in child form, she wanted him to know that wasn't how she really was. He might have left it there but something in him kept going, not seeming to notice, or maybe not to care, that Agata was trying her best not to cry.

All the while, Melody would not offer her stepdaughter support, in fact she seemed to mentally diverge, diving deeper and deeper into her drawing, as if she might press the pen through sand and end up somewhere else.

'Are you OK?' Gail whispered to Agata. 'Is there anything I can do?'

'Stay out of it,' sniffed Agata.

'She isn't wrong,' said Ezra. Melody lifted her head from the table.

'Here,' said Gail, trying to re-set. 'This is my idea. Just based on what you're describing.'

She passed a sketch to Melody, who pulled it closer and closer to her eyes until it looked for a moment like she might insert it into her eyeballs.

'I LOVE IT.'

Melody held it up for the others to see: a delicate ink sketch of an octopus who had wrapped, in each tentacle, a rose.

Ezra shifted in his chair. 'Won't people think your perfume smells of fish?'

'NO,' said Melody. 'They'll understand that it's a rose scent that changes shape *and* that there's nothing else like it on the planet.' She kissed Gail's hand. Then she swept the napkin off the table and folded it into her suede handbag.

Ezra made the 'cheque, please' sign at the waiter and the waiter had to come over and explain it had already been covered. Shaking, the waiter pointed at Gail.

Ezra turned to her. 'You paid for this?'

'Yes,' she said, trying to project confidence, 'as a little thank-you for everything you guys have done for me since we met.'

'It wasn't a little bill. You can't afford it.'

He was starting to lose his iron grip on the table. He had no grip on Gail at all.

This girl, it hit him plain as day, *is a liability.*

Ezra got up and went up to talk to the maitre d.

'What you have done,' spat Agata, shocked because she didn't know she could still produce spit, 'is so fucking insulting to my father. He's back there trying to reverse it, and to fix what you've done.'

Gail was taken aback by the energy, and Agata seemed slightly taken aback, too, by the power of her voice, by the force with which she shook her thin fingers at her new friend.

'That's crazy,' is all Gail said.

'Idiot!' spat Agata, an anger there for all the things she'd held back over the two years of her illness, when she was being quiet and still and refined and guided by others.

'Who do you think you are?' she asked Gail.

Melody's head was back on the table.

'You're only angry because he's angry,' said Gail, trying to remain steady. 'If he were happy, you'd be happy. You don't have anything of your own.'

'Why are you here?' Agata said, and then she pressed one bony finger into Gail, and they both looked at it, the indent it made in Gail's soft flesh. 'Why are you even here?'

'You invited me!'

'Actually, I don't think that I did. I think you invited yourself and thought I was too weak and too frail to notice.'

'Maybe you were.'

'Fuck you,' said Agata.

Now Gail felt nervous.

Agata got up and left. Ezra refused to look at Gail as he worked over the card machine and the maitre d shook at his visible fury.

For a moment it was just her and Ezra, under the deco windows, an ornate chandelier hanging down, casting shadows across their shadow where it had felt, earlier that evening, to be casting warm light on their glowing skin.

She said it again: 'That's crazy.'

Ezra would not so much as look at her, the quiet rage pulsing through his veins visible to the naked eye, and there were scores of eyes on them.

'I didn't mean to do anything wrong.'

She walked to the limo and saw Agata already inside it.

'You can't come back to our hotel.'

'Why not?'

She began to feel a creeping sense of dread, like getting under your duvet to feel, on your bare skin, something that could be cookie crumbs, but could be spider eggs.

Ezra approached behind her.

'We need some family time. I've booked you a seat on the last Eurostar tonight.'

She tried to make him understand:

'I don't think I did anything wrong. I don't understand why you're all freaking out. Sorry if I come from a different world.' She hated how her voice sounded high, like the floor she and Dar lived on. You can say you have an epic view, but at the end of the day, you still live on the top floor because it's cheaper there.

Ezra touched her upper arm, once, quickly, and she flinched before he even said the words: 'It's just not done. It's insulting.' He exhaled. 'And you were making Melody nervous with the Hebrew prayer that wouldn't end.'

'Why?'

'Well, she felt left out. She couldn't understand, she felt excluded, like you were trying to have something she couldn't be a part of.'

Though that was what she had been trying to do, she denied it furiously.

'I would never try to exclude her. She's your wife!' As if everything wasn't everything and they didn't both know that. The greater unsaid was that Agata, the reason they'd been brought together, didn't really count, that she had no bearing on much of anything. That her father had wept and sobbed for her health and the possibility of her death. But now she was on the path to improvement, Agata held little power over him.

'I helped Agata though. Didn't I?'

He looked at her in the limo.

'She would have grown out of it.'

'Yeah. Right. Like given enough time Melody's clothes

are going to get out of the red and turn a profit.' Bitter, pointed dart. He didn't let her see him flinch, let her think it – she – was just a mosquito bite. She didn't want to see him sunken in on himself like that. That wasn't what she wanted from him.

Now her voice was small. 'I did that for you.'

'Hey,' he took her arm. 'Do you understand what *I* did for *you*?'

'I think so.'

He got into the limo without asking her to join.

'Where shall I go until my train? I don't know this city.'

'Just go straight to the station. You are a strong and capable girl.' He looked over at the women in the back seat of the limo, one high, one furious. 'That's what I like about you.' He handed her money for a taxi.

In the limo, Ezra dwelled on the interaction with the waiter and realised he had not raised his voice to his daughter in a very long time. The threat of her fragile mental health curtailed any regular paternal interaction, any ability to reprimand her in any way. He felt how much he'd missed it.

PART 6

CHAPTER 30

Ezra had been detached since they'd got back from Amsterdam – he'd still kiss Melody's forehead when he entered whatever room she was in but had stopped coming to her before bed. She tried to figure out what she might have done wrong on the trip but could think of nothing, only how nice it had been to all be together. She dimly remembered him snapping at Agata on the last night, but he'd probably just been tired. She could see things more clearly when he fucked her. Without his largeness pushing inside her at night to make her feel small in the world, she lost her grasp of details.

Rejected, she fell back on the tiny repetitive movements of sewing a dress from scratch. She didn't question him on it but, if there was to be no sex, she'd simply go all the way, a needle-and-thread spinster in an attic (a very nice attic bedroom). She'd create the work herself as she had when he first fell for her. Maybe by the time it was done he would touch her again. She sewed at strange hours, when childhood nightmares kicked in and she'd found long ago she was better off just getting up and working.

Very often she was high, the needle moving in and out of the fabric with a sly, speedy coldness that, for all the lack of physical affection, turned her on. She'd studied Comme des Garçons Spring/Summer 1997 for the daring placement of lumps and bulges (every serious fashion designer had, and whatever people thought of her, she counted herself as one of them). She knew critics would pick up the reference and she didn't mind – enough time had passed that it was an homage and not a rip-off.

Eventually she handed her design over to the old ladies in the East End, aware that there was a construction element required that was beyond the capabilities of her late-night needle and thread. Still, she travelled all the way to Whitechapel to check on the outfit's progression as the days went on and the launch of her perfume drew closer. To the old ladies' chagrin, she had them at one point unpick and replace the foam with the same kind used in Ezra's sixty-thousand-pound mattress. The ladies looked up at her, at first shaking their heads at the avant-garde task they'd been assigned by the silly young wife of a man with too much money. But as they got deeper into it, they became as invested in the dress as she was, gently testing the capability of the foam appendages, as if teaching their own child to walk.

It went on like this until they'd done all eight pieces of the gown and attached them with invisible needle work. Melody jumped back in each day for the final haul – sitting beside the old ladies, all of them sewing the pearls, row by row, priceless and glistening, the creamy ones against the black spattering, obscene, as they were intended to be.

When it was time to try it on, an old lady on either side of Melody, they all looked in the mirror and gasped.

It didn't matter that Ezra was too messed up about poor Terry to make love to her any more: she felt turned on when she saw her reflection. Pressing the fabric against her body, dreaming into it. She knew now, looking in the mirror at this, her most painstaking piece, that she was gifted, and that he was right to have backed her. If he was losing money on her ventures, that was the public's fault, not hers.

By the next week Gail's erotic thoughts about Ezra would not stop. They interfered with her lessons, and her ability to navigate bus journeys she'd been on a hundred times so she got off at wrong stops or on to the wrong bus completely.

Waiting on the Tube platform, she had bent to pet a woman's dog – politely asking if it was OK to do so – realising too late that it was not a dog but a bunch of flowers. At the local café, on her lunch break, she was charmed that the greasy spoon had found her mature enough to bring her a choice of red and white wine with her chips, before understanding that one was a bottle of ketchup and the other mayonnaise.

She tried texting Ezra and got nothing.

She thought she was still taking her medication at the right time, but sometimes she missed a dose or accidentally took two at once. She forgot to refill her prescription and had to go three days without any as Dar pleaded with the pharmacy to rectify her daughter's mistake.

On the days she had run out, she sat down to write a letter to George Michael, as it usually helped her to try to help him. But she only got as far as:

Dear George,
    I've been praying that things are feeling more
hopeful for you . . .

But she hadn't been; she'd thought of him far less than normal.

Trying to clear her head with a long walk on the Heath, she imagined she could see George pulling a man off behind a tree. But even in her private imagination, she felt she must not watch and so she moved her field of imagined vision further through the park, to the families packing up their picnics.

She put the pen down, wadded up the latest letter to George and, lying on her back in the grass, she ate her words.

In the final week of November, the weather had turned extremely cold and so had Agata. When Gail would see her, she'd turn her face, her curtain of blonde hair a sign saying 'SORRY, WE ARE CLOSED'. One day, despite her best manoeuvring not to be in Gail's energy field, she was in front of her in line at the cafeteria.

'Hey. How are you? If you ever want to talk?' Gail said gently.

'I don't want to talk.'

'But if you *did* want to?'

'I don't.'

'Look. I really don't understand what happened,' Gail said as the line began to move, Christmas decorations hanging above them.

'Because you aren't well in the head.'

'*I'm* not well? You can talk.'

Then, suddenly, Agata pushed Gail against the wall. She had strength in her. It was incredible. Gail might have clapped if Agata hadn't immediately hissed:

'I know about you and my father.'

CHAPTER *31*

Melody intended to be in her very best shape for the launch of the scent and had researched her path to this as carefully as she had the scent components. There had been discussions with three different doctors about scarring. Who could leave the thinnest scars hidden in the most inventive places? Who included sessions in a hyperbaric oxygen chamber post-surgery?

'If anything shows, which it won't, you'd just wear your hair down,' said one.

'You see,' said another doctor (not just a world-class surgeon but an actual Professor of Scars) as he traced his finger inside the curl of Melody's ear, 'we tuck it away in there.' It was the most intimately she'd been touched in a while, since Ezra had retreated from her physically.

The scar issue was of particular importance since she'd fully intended to get the procedure done weeks ago, but had to cancel and reschedule her surgery when the incident with Terry took place. Terry remained in a coma and so, in a sense, did her marriage. At least this would give her something she'd be able to recover from.

*

Dar was increasingly shaken by the events at the hospital where, in lieu of any actual improvement in Terry Loft's condition, photographers had sneaked in to take a photo of him hooked up to the machines. The failure of the hospital security caused her to examine her own defence system.

The credit card bill had arrived from Gail's Amsterdam restaurant incident and Dar couldn't imagine how to pay it off, except by meeting the minimum due each month. It never even crossed her mind that, because it was Gail's fuck-up, Gail should get a Saturday job to try to make amends.

That night, at 1am her anxiety about it was such that Dar gave up trying to sleep and went to Gail's bedroom, where her daughter was asleep with the duvet pulled up to her nose against the encroaching December chill.

'No, Mum. I'm tired.' Dar didn't move. 'Mum?'

'Can I be with you?' Dar asked.

'Mum. You're OK on your own.'

She was silent in the dark.

'It's frightened me, what happened today, with Terry.'

Gail sat up, and spoke to her as kindly and as gently as she could muster.

'I don't think it's that bad. Tabloids are tabloids. It's just what they do.'

'He looks so vulnerable with all those wires. He's just a kid. I've started to wonder what really happened. What does Agata think?'

Stiffening, Gail opened her eyes but didn't turn to face her, saying: 'Kids today are mixed up in all sorts of things.

We don't know what it was that got him where he is.
Every time I saw him, he was just a silly little pisshead.'

'He's a human being.'

'Mum. Please don't worry.' She sat up, pulling the
duvet close.

Dar stopped herself crying until she didn't and then
two tears rolled down her face and she didn't scoop them
up like hummus and eat them the way she had to Gail
when she was a kid.

'Why are you crying, Mum?'

'Dad fled here from such terrible things and . . . even
though what he went through didn't happen to me, when
something really wrong happens in the world, I feel it all
light up in me. You'd have been too young to notice. But
I've never been so close to something as awful as this.
Hearing the constant beep beep beep and his mum there
holding his hand day in, day out. I can't ever calm down.'

Gail took her mother and walked her back to her own
room. She helped her into the bed, tucked her under the
sheet and waited until she was drifting off. As she went
to turn off the bedside light Dar whispered: 'Leave it on.'

'You said it wastes electricity?'

'Please leave it on.'

The next day came an offer that righted things and reduced
the anxiety that buzzed through Dar like a speedball.

Melody called Gail and said she had a small procedure the next day and that her regular home nurse had
fallen through, having been unexpectedly deported to the
Philippines. She asked if perhaps her mother might be
interested in the job.

'Does Agata know you were going to call me?'

'What do you mean?' answered Melody, and whether she was genuinely unaware of their falling-out or pretending to be ignorant for convenience was debatable.

Dar, in bits about the credit card bill and wanting to escape the terrible atmosphere at the hospital, agreed to take the job.

CHAPTER 32

Dar booked five days off work. On the fifth day Melody's stitches would be removed and she had enough experience to manage from there herself. But up to that day, the care she received would affect her health on the macro level – she could get a blood infection – but on the micro, it would affect the formation of the scar. This part thrilled and fascinated Melody – the mystery of what she had done being contained behind a thin white line that would become, with proper treatment, a sealed confidence. Hiring Dar gave the patient and nurse the accelerated intimacy of being in on a secret. And unlike mere gossip or rumour, it was a secret that could be revealed and inspected.

The truth was, Melody did know that Gail and Agata were no longer friends. She didn't like it when people fell out, it made her sad. It was a way to keep it going, having the mother here. But she was also being kind, wasn't she? Throwing a bone to this poor single mother. And she was curious about her. What sort of woman raised a girl like Gail? Agata didn't know what she was losing! Agata, she felt if she were truly honest, wasn't good enough to see what quality of friend she'd had in Gail.

She thought her stepdaughter had made an inexplicable, rash decision, so didn't even bother telling her about Dar being in their home. Agata was oblivious, anyway, in her own world. She had a new set, and mainly spent time with Faith. She was testing the volume controls on choosing life instead of death now she was almost at a normal weight for her age, turning them up and down, searching for the right frequency to stick with.

It was a leap for Melody, admitting the 'truth' of the operation to someone who knew her, and Dar sort of kind of knew her by extension. As usual, she would *never* talk about it with her husband. Ezra always knew it was happening but treated it as Victorian men did childbirth. He waited far away until it was over, but then cooed over the result.

Only porn stars and Real Housewives actually talked about what they had done to their faces and bodies, and they did it so they could monetise. Melody didn't need any money so it all stayed private.

Dar decided that Gail could stay alone in the flat while she was looking after Melody.

'I'm not coming with you?' asked Gail, astounded.

'Of course not.'

It made her wild inside to imagine her mother in their world and she still up in the flat. Five whole days in there! Imagine what you could lift up and find! She tried to stay calm.

'Can I visit you?'

But Dar was calmer. 'I don't think that's really appropriate.'

'*Why?*'

'Well, it would be unprofessional.'

'The job wouldn't have happened without me.'

'The credit card bill wouldn't have happened without you.'

Then she hugged Gail and put a cordon around her tantrum. 'Listen. I'm so looking forward to a change. I can feel it's a good thing, honey. So thank you.'

When Agata saw Dar in the house, she didn't even connect that this was Gail's mother, just recognised her on sight as another helper being helpful. Agata saw that as a great quality of Melody's: that she knew what they needed help with and how to get it in a way that surpassed the mere hiring of servants. That Melody always felt better for the tenderness with which the housekeeper folded the laundry and the care she used to find the most sensitive possible detergent. This latest woman, Agata could see from the landing as she entered, was very much Melody's style.

The girl pulled back from the banisters without saying a word and stayed in her own bedroom on the top floor, texting Faith. The house was perfectly big enough to maintain separate worlds.

Dar was in a single bed opposite Melody so she could watch her progress intently, a botanist taking a rare orchid home from work. Ezra was off on a business trip, one of many scheduled once the detectives came calling about Terry. Within his home, he made it seem this latest had been timed this way very deliberately because of Melody's paranoia of Ezra seeing her in the immediate aftermath. But someone had to be watching for the first twenty-four hours after anaesthesia, to make sure there were no complications. For a few hours, tubes in her nose to maintain her breathing, she and Terry Loft had been in the same parallel dimension.

Melody loved going under, knowing everything was about to be taken out of her control and she could rest. Most people who commit suicide just want to be left to rest for a very long time. The luxury of her multiple plastic surgeries was not just how much better she felt she looked, but that she got to do mini monitored suicides without anyone feeling betrayed. She generally came out of the anaesthesia crying like a little baby, and she always loved that part, it felt so good, the flow of tears down her frozen face that she absolutely could not feel but someone always bent to mop up.

This time it was Dar.

'There, there,' she said, as Melody sniffled.

Dar hadn't been shocked at the sight of her when she arrived to pick her up from the private hospital; she'd seen a lot worse. But it was strange that this was the very first time she was seeing the famous beauty's face and the face was utterly destroyed, swollen purple and glossy and smelling foul.

Once they were home, Dar placed ice over Melody's eyes and painstakingly drained the fluid that had gathered either side of her jaw. She'd never minded changing Gail's nappies. Even that had moved her because it meant her baby was a real working human, functioning correctly.

Both shattered in their own ways, Dar and Melody slept in sync through the night. In the morning Dar woke up, gave Melody her painkiller and asked the cook if she might wait in the bedroom for half an hour while she took a walk to the grocery store. She took in the air and smiled at locals and bought a coffee from Panzer's that was bitter because it was too expensive and had been over-roasted.

Melody slowly opened her eyes as Dar re-entered the bedroom.

'You know,' she whispered to Dar, her throat scratchy from a tube, 'you have really beautiful skin.'

Did Dar know that? Maybe, once. She hadn't done any intervention and it was supple and only wrinkled where she'd really used it, to frown deeply and smile broadly, and she could live just fine with that.

'Where are you from exactly?'

Oh. Melody had meant the *colour* of her skin. This happened sometimes. It was a fifty/fifty shot whether it was meant in admiration or as a dig. It had been useful at the marches being non-specifically other. Even when she was marching with the Jewish Bloc, they'd mainly thought she was Palestinian. That was how he first got talking to her. He'd also had to approach because the message she had written on her placard was so long-winded and obtuse, in such small letters, that he had to come right next to her to read it.

'You have a really strong physique,' Melody continued.

Something about the word 'physique' felt like a grandma staring too close at your body. She forgave Melody because she looked so beat up.

'Do you weight train?' Melody continued.

'I march.'

'Like a marching band?'

'No. I go on a protest most weekends.'

'You protest?' Melody tried to sit up on her pillows. 'What about? In particular?'

'Hush now, you need to rest.'

Melody's eyes felt sticky with Vaseline. 'I'm just interested.'

'If I tell you will you rest?'

'Yes,' Melody promised.

'Save the NHS. Black Lives Matter. Vote for Jeremy Corbyn. Free Palestine.'

'Vote against Brexit?'

'Well, if that's what the people want, I don't really get involved in that one. It's not a priority for Jeremy, he has so much else on his plate.'

Dar said 'Jeremy' in the same way she spoke of her daughter — like she knew him better than she really did and also like she was expecting too much from him.

'Let's not talk about this, swallow your medicine.'

Even in her haze, Melody knew this was not quite right. She was talented but also quite stupid, and that could be a potent combination. Maybe you have to be anaesthetised to get by — Marlon Brando by over-eating, say — if you are talented but dumb.

Dar turned on the TV to distract Melody, as if she were a child under her feet rather than a billionaire housewife paying her to tend her plastic surgery recovery so her husband wouldn't have to.

Still, Dar was very soft with Melody. She was able to focus on the healing of the wounds, and it pleased her to do a good job. Whether or not this woman was vain, she convinced herself to hyper-fixate and soon she was enjoying herself.

She could judge their values all she liked (and she did). But she enjoyed bringing Melody her tea in bed and getting such a generous 'thank you', the stream of cooing compliments about how kind she was, how needed. On the second evening, when she adjusted the television for her, Melody said, 'Oh, I'm having the best time with you! You are so much fun!'

CHAPTER 33

Ezra returned from his trip three days sooner than he'd been meant to at the behest of his lawyer, who had negotiated terms of a sit down with the Loft detective. Three days makes all the difference in a cosmetic surgery recovery.

He came home at midnight, jet-lagged and confused and, still, on edge. The cook came out in her dressing gown and offered to whip him up an omelette, but he sent her away. First he ate pretzels from the pantry, then he opened the door of the fridge that contained only drinks, and drained a few cans of beer.

Then, with a slight alcohol buzz in him, feeling finally a little horny and sad, Ezra climbed the stairs to get into bed with his wife. Not finding her in their quarters, he assumed she was staying in her own bedroom tonight, and he was right.

He opened the door without knocking and at the sound of this, his wife – or what he took to be his wife, since the mess of purple meat had her hair and nail polish – sat up in bed.

'Jesus fucking Christ,' Ezra gasped.

Melody took a sticky moment to open her vaselined eyes, and when she was able to focus, when she saw it was her husband standing before her, she let out a blood-curdling scream, far, far more triggered than if it had been a stranger.

He held onto the brass at the end of her bed in order to steady himself.

'I'm sorry,' he whispered, 'I'm sorry.'

He swallowed. He'd never gone to look, had always respected her privacy to heal in secret, then reappeared when she was ready. And now he understood. And he understood that this was a mistake that could not be undone.

Melody had screamed so loud, and it was her scream combined with the terrible bruising, swelling, sutures and drains that rendered her truly a monster. 'I'm sorry, sweetheart,' he said, 'I'm sorry, we got done early and I just – I forgot.'

'Hello,' said Dar, looking up from a seat by the window. She wore an unofficial nurse's uniform purchased from a medical outlet. Had she been there all the time?

'I'm her nurse,' Dar explained, 'I'm Dar.' But he just apologised again. Like her daughter, she had met him at a rare moment when he was vulnerable.

'Hi,' he said, looking at the ground. He knew exactly who this woman was, could see it right away. How had Gail managed to implant her mother here?

The bad feeling was spreading through him like poison. He hadn't felt like this in such a long time. He sat in his office for almost an hour, shaking. He hadn't felt like this since way back when.

Though she was still crushed at being ignored by not one but two Levys, Gail enjoyed having the flat to herself. She'd fallen asleep in her clothes several nights. She'd taken three baths a day, addicted to the womb-like feeling. Now she was going through drawers in her mum's room. She tried on Dar's makeup. She used the very last spritz of the perfume from the bathroom, and then she slept in her mum's bed. She noticed properly for the first time that her mum's room did not have anywhere near as pretty a view as hers, in fact her window was facing a wall. It was smaller too. But still, she liked the transgression.

When she woke up it was Sunday and she had nothing to do but keep opening drawers. It was in the bottom left-hand corner of what she'd thought was a stationery cabinet that she noticed the envelope. Inside was an X-ray of a skull, which, the natural light that morning being a classical London grey, she switched on the lamp to examine.

She wasn't meant to show up at the Levys' while her mum was working. She didn't even need to promise – it had been a given. When the security presented her to Dar, she hustled Gail into the sitting room attached to Melody's bedroom.

Ezra's office was one floor away from his wife. Gail didn't even care if either of them were home or not. But Dar saw her eyes darting and said, 'They're not here. They went to a movie.' Ezra had tried to stay out of the house entirely since the terrible event. 'What are you doing here?'

She pushed the envelope towards her mother.

'What did Grandpa die of? It wasn't just old age.'

Dar sat down on the sofa.

'I don't like to talk about it.'

'I'm sorry, Mum,' she opened the envelope, 'but can we?'

'It's all so awful.'

She knelt in front of Dar, holding her hands in hers. 'I can take it.'

'Why are you asking me now?'

'I opened a drawer I wasn't meant to.'

'Because you can't accept that not everything is yours.' Dar's eyes blazed. 'That some parts of the flat are mine!' She meant, 'Some parts of me are mine!'

'I'm really sorry, Mum. But in here I found a hospital X-ray with your dad's name on it. Can you explain it to me?' She slid out the X-ray and passed it to Dar.

Dar stood up to check on Melody but Gail said, 'She's out cold,' and sat her back down. Dar held the X-ray envelope in her hands without looking at it.

'Mum?'

Dar put her hands over her eyes when she finally answered. 'The government wouldn't let them emigrate to Palestine because they didn't want there to be a Jewish state. One day, policemen woke him and his brother and said their watches were spy radios to Zionists. The policemen took their watches and turned him and his brother in.'

'But he got out?'

'Yes.' Her voice cracked.

'Someone from the resistance paid a bribe and they were able to get him permission to leave for Tel Aviv. The airport was brand new and beautiful and he'd never seen one before, never been outside Iraq. On his way out, the airport staff beat him before they let him board the plane. He got to Tel Aviv. They gave him great medical care. But he had trouble with the head injury his whole life. And in the end, even all those decades later, it was ultimately the thing that did him in.'

Still holding her mother's hands, Gail looked at Dar a long time.

'Why do you protest outside the embassy?'

'What?'

Melody turned in her sleep.

'Why do you want an end to the country that gave your father refuge? How is that the hill you've chosen to die on?'

'I have a lot of hills. I have a strong belief system . . . quiet, you'll wake her.'

'She can take it. She's married to a Jew!'

'The worst kind!' spat Dar. 'The worst! One who makes it harder for the rest of us to live in peace no matter what country we go to!'

Melody stirred. 'Dar?'

'Yes. I'm here.' She stood up and was at her side.

'Are you talking to someone, Dar?'

'No,' Dar said, staring her daughter down. She put the X-ray back in the envelope and sealed it, then she went into the bathroom and splashed water on her face

Hearing the sound of the taps, Gail moved as quickly and quietly as a cat. She passed into the sitting room of Melody's bedroom, where she knew Marilyn Monroe's certificate of conversion had been hung. She stood on her tiptoes, felt for the hook, and took it off the wall. She figured there were probably cameras all over the house. But not in the bedroom. Even from here, she could hear Melody's breathing was heavy but steady.

'Dar? Dar?' Melody called.

Hearing this, Gail carefully put the certificate back on the wall. Her mother still in the bathroom, Gail went to Melody's side.

'Dar?'

Gail answered, 'Yes. Here I am.' *Hineni.*

'I need more painkillers, Dar.'

'Of course,' Gail said, reaching for the vial.

Gail put it to Melody's lips and handed her the cup of water, tipping her head. She heard Dar drying her hands.

'You are such a wonderful person. Gail is so lucky to have you as a mother.'

Gail backed out of the room, as you are supposed to do if menaced by a shark.

On her way out of the house, she saw, on the kitchen table, a box marked MELODY but with a logo of octopus tentacles and roses. The return label was an Amsterdam address. She couldn't help herself, but what teenager has impulse control? She carefully unsealed it. Inside was the first prototype of the finished perfume. Her mum's scent that she usually used had run out. And this had all been her idea, hadn't it? Everyone owed her, as far as she was concerned, every single person in this fucking house had something to thank her for. This could be a form of reparation. She slipped it into her pocket and left.

CHAPTER 34

Gail detoured past George Michael's to see if a light was on. If it had been, it's not that she wouldn't have rung the bell. But she might have just sat on the nearby bench and meditated a while. But the house, though the curtains were not closed, sat in darkness.

When she reached their flat, she went to put the key in the top lock of her front door, but found it was already ajar. She called out, 'Hello? Hello?' Then she tiptoed inside.

Ezra was standing stock still in the middle of the kitchen, a phone against his ear. He hung up slowly when he saw her. She was so pleased to finally see him again, she could have cried.

'Were you at my house just now?' he asked slowly.

'Who are you talking to? Why are you here?'

'Why were you *there*?'

He walked over and shut the still-open front door. The care with which he closed it, so no sound was made, flicked a switch in her.

'I don't think you should be here . . . my mother will be back . . .' she trailed off.

'No, she won't, because she's with my wife. As you know. Because you probably put her there.'

'Like hell I did.'

'And because you were just there.'

'Well, she'll be here soon, so she can tell you herself, it was nothing to do with me.'

He looked away, ran his hand through his thick hair. 'I think we both know you're way beyond being protected by your mother any more.' Then he looked back, as she tried not to squirm.

'What are you on about? Hey, it's nice to see you finally.'

He didn't answer.

'This is a fucked-up game of chess.' She smiled.

'You don't know how to play chess though, because you're not as smart as you think.' He came closer.

She was so surprised to have him in her space, her senses were off, heightened but registering the information incorrectly. Was she scared? She searched the pockets of her body for the feeling. And then it struck her . . . was *he* scared?

'What did you touch when you were in my house?'

'What did I touch?' She had put Marilyn's certificate back on the wall almost the moment she'd lifted it off. 'I don't know what you're talking about.'

'You fucking spy,' he said, shaking his head. 'Did you open anything that wasn't for you?'

She stared him down, silent and stony, back straightened, channelling an Olympic gymnast before they mount the pommel horse.

'Just tell me the truth, Gail.' He put on a pair of gloves. The little hairs on the back of her neck, the hairs Dar loved to kiss when she was a toddler, they all stood on end.

'You opened a package that had the prototype of Melody's perfume.'

'Yes. I was just curious.' Her voice sounded to her like it was being thrown across the room by a ventriloquist.

'Give it to me.' His was sonorous, as if coming from deep inside a cave.

'I was only curious because it was my idea to do it. I just wanted to smell it.'

He came closer still. 'Have you opened the bottle?'

'Not yet.'

'Have you touched it?' He laid a gloved hand on the back of a chair.

'I put it in my pocket.'

He took another step towards her and placed his gloved hand into her pocket. She could feel him on her, his sleepy lion breath.

'Don't hurt me.'

'You stupid girl. You don't know what you took. I'm here because I'm saving you. *Again*.'

'What are you talking about? I'm saving you! That's always been what I was doing!'

He grimaced as he held the glass bottle. 'This isn't what it says it is.'

She stood her ground. 'It came from the nose in Amsterdam.'

'I. Don't. Think. So. We weren't expecting it yet.'

She shivered. 'Then what is it?'

'I think it's something that could kill you.' He nodded his head, in agreement with himself. 'You're going to have to take your clothes off.'

'No!'

'Yes.'

Then instead of moving towards her, he moved further away and sat down. This made his insistence far worse. 'Take them off and put them in that bag I've put over there.'

'Who else is here?' She pulled her arms around her, as Lilah had when Dar had forced everyone to be invited to the pool party, which felt as far in the past as to be another life.

'No one. It's just us.'

'Why are there no bodyguards with you?'

'It's too dangerous. I don't want to risk killing them too. Look, I have it on good authority and I have to take it seriously. A lot's been shaken up lately. As you well know. There have been a lot of threats.' He sat back in the chair. 'I have enemies. People who haven't been able to move on or change the way I have. People who can't leave the past behind.'

He wasn't going to leave the flat and her mother wasn't going to come home. She didn't know what else to do.

So she took off her clothes, very slowly. There was no mirror in front of her, but still she felt turned on as she did it, the fear draining from her with each layer removed. He collected each item with his gloved hand, depositing them in the plastic bag, which he then sealed tightly, moving away from it. When she was naked, he didn't look at her body.

'You need to shower head to toe,' he said, 'and scrub, and wash your hair.'

'You only wash curly hair twice a week and I've done it already.'

'*Wash your hair.*' He sounded like a stern father. 'Which bathroom here has the shower?'

'There's only one bathroom. We share it.'

He followed her there. She got in the shower, him standing on the other side of the glass, his arms crossed.

'Why are you standing there?'

'I need to know you've gotten it done. I don't want it on my conscience and I don't want it leading back to me.'

Gail turned on the water and said, '*Got* it done. It's not gotten.'

'Get on with it!'

'I'm waiting for it to heat up!'

When she was finished, she stepped out, took the towel he was holding out for her, and wrapped herself in it.

'Thanks for trusting me,' he said, still not looking at her.

'You're welcome.'

He wagged his finger at her, as if he could refashion all that had passed between them in the last half-hour as a Hanna-Barbera cartoon. 'Don't touch other people's stuff. Are you crying? Don't cry.'

She was stony. 'I've got shampoo in my eyes.'

He still had his gloves on as he dabbed a towel across her eyes, very, very gently, and as he did he triggered the word; it tumbled out of her before she could stop it:

'Daddy?'

He could have said:

'Yes, baby?'

He could have taken off the plastic glove and put his thumb in her mouth. He could have put her thumb in *his* mouth. He could have held her and told her he didn't feel that way about her, or even that he *did* feel that way, but that it was his job as an adult to protect her from hormonal teenage obsessions that could harm her.

But he did not respond at all. He merely gathered everything and walked past her.

At the door, he threw her a capsule.

'Take this pill.'

Catching it, she looked at it in her palm.

'Why?'

'It's an antidote.'

'To what?'

'To all of it.'

After he left, she cried for a long time. She made great hiccupping sobbing sounds in a way she never could have done if her mother were not out of the flat. And when she was done crying she took the shower head from its holder and made different animal sounds. She thought: *So this is what sex is for. It's there to combat the great, unyielding shame and sorrow.*

She pictured the view across the Heath, where men would be making their way across the tall grasses, leaning behind trees, on their knees, in groups and one on one, some faces covered, some bold as brass, all reaching for immortality.

Thank God. Thank God for desire, she thought. She'd have many great loves as she grew up, but she usually thought of him wiping her eyes when she came, even if he were just a cameo, a wave from behind a net curtain in the backdrop of her fantasies.

And, by the morning, Terry Loft's miracle recovery was the headline in every paper – alive but rendered forever a child.

<h1 style="text-align:center">CHAPTER 35</h1>

That weekend, when Melody awoke from her deep, long sleep, she remembered, again, that he had seen her, that he had gone into the attic and found the picture of Dorian Gray. Her stomach lurched and her heart felt like it would break and those two things were undignified in combination. Either the heartache or stomach lurch ought to be removed before leaving the house, as per Coco Chanel's maxim about excessive accessories. But there was no way to unclasp your internal organs and place them delicately in your jewellery box. So she'd better just stay in bed. Until she could forgive him his intrusion. Until she was herself. Her regular, resilient, optimistic, hopeful self.

He did love her. He did protect her and believe in her. It wasn't just about her beauty. A great man. A kind man. A man who wouldn't hurt a fly, who went out of his way to help people in need. She'd learn to get over his mistake. They'd be all right. She could roll out the scent line to include a hair mist and a luxury deodorant! There. She started to feel like this was manageable.

And then she remembered the look of horror on his face. She remembered how she couldn't stop screaming, how guttural it had been, violently expelling everything she'd ever held in over the years of their marriage. There was only one thing to do. Take more of her pain killers.

She slept deeply again and when she awoke, flustered and with sweat beneath her breasts, she didn't understand that only twenty minutes had passed. She hadn't quite kept track. She thought she had. It's just that she'd got it wrong. So she took another pill. That could happen to anyone.

Melody had first the lovely woozy feeling that happened each time. If she was unlucky there was nausea. But when she got lucky – and mainly she had been lucky – there was the wave to ride of peace and happiness.

She wanted an orange and ginger juice from Panzer's deli. If she could just have that, she'd feel OK again. She wished that Dar were still there. Usually Melody forgot about helpers after they'd stopped helping and their cheque had been cut. Maybe it was Dar leaving so suddenly, on Ezra's return, that had lodged her in Melody's mind. She had helped her heal so the surgery was imperceptible. Still, Ezra having seen her in that ugly, transitional moment grew in her mind like a keloid scar.

Melody wobbled into a cream coat, too high to close any of the buttons correctly. She wandered past the hospital where Agata had been an inpatient all those weeks. She remembered that she'd been jealous of her, getting to stay there and be taken care of. She had watched them administer a sedative one night and felt so envious, though she had known there were things about herself the girl envied. It is so painful to think that you are not going to be more beautiful than your mother. She did remember how excited she'd been herself, at Agata's age, when she'd understood she'd overtake her mother in looks.

She walked past Panzer's with its two-state solution where wealthy Arabs and Jews sat beside each other without acknowledging each other's presence. At the juice stall, she asked for her special juice. She held it to her lips but she couldn't quite feel her lips, so it dribbled. She didn't see that it had hit her cream cashmere coat. If she had known, and if she were herself, she would have taken it off right there in the street; better to be half naked than visibly stained. She hadn't worn heels, she had on luxurious sheepskin-lined boots, so falling wasn't an issue with the painkiller.

It was really cold now Christmas was upon them. The sky was so blue and the clouds were huge and heavy but unobstructive, arranged in formation like the band on the cover of an album. Blue sky on a cold day was such a gift, and it made her think of when she was a little girl in Poland. How she envied the neighbour's pony so much, she'd brush the pony through a fence with a long brush. Then leaving childhood and becoming a teenager and the men in the village staring. And they had never stopped.

So she was not, now, attuned when people were staring at her for the wrong reasons, as she wobbled and weaved.

Suddenly, she wanted to go home, needed to be in her bed. She walked back towards the house, until she found herself stuck among the tourists of the Abbey Road crossing. They had each waited their turn to cross the road, a lava crust of politeness in a world on fire. When you're out of line with society, it doesn't matter if you're beautiful, in fact that makes it worse. If you are ugly or dull people can look away from your transgression. But she was just so beautiful. Some tourists tried to nudge her politely as she walked into their shots. But this was just a crossing, wasn't it? she thought. She had forgotten all about the Beatles.

With the double – or was it triple? Quadruple dose? – she had forgotten a lot of things, all body, no thought. Thank God. Thank God. Cars honked at her. She could see her home in the distance, the top of it where Agata rode her lift to. The very top, the fifth floor. But maybe she just thought she could see it.

Agata has been taking the stairs, they'd started saying to each other as they'd realised something was wrong with her step-daughter, that she'd cut her calories and upped her exercise and lost a lot of weight. When she'd started getting sick, they'd noticed that she didn't use the lift to get to her bedroom any more.

Agata had spent so many years dying so slowly for so long, and her stepmother did not die right away either. The motorist who hit her kept driving until he was apprehended.

Melody was visible, still alive, in some photos, when they were examined – standing at the back of the line as Lennon, in others weaving into second place as McCartney. At the time, the tourists thought she'd ruined their pictures but then, as things unfolded, they became sick artefacts, ones that the tabloids paid good money for.

The secondary line of storytelling in the papers was the diamonds that had been removed from her ears, so many tiny little diamonds that you can see how someone in the ambulance or at the hospital or in the morgue or maybe a fast-moving stranger at the scene had thought nobody would notice if a few of them were gone. But Ezra noticed. Because Ezra always, *always* counted his blessings, individually and meticulously.

Before the life drained from her, the last thing Melody saw as she lay on the crosswalk was groups of four, satelliting each other, and, because she had forgotten all about the Beatles, she thought everywhere she looked were nuclear family units.

CHAPTER 36

Melody's death knocked from the papers the tragedy of the once-starry young footballer who'd live the rest of his life as a child. And pointed any lingering finger of guilt away from Ezra, since he had now suffered a terrible loss, one captured on amateur lenses. The lurid bright colours of the event made it easier to empathise with him. The interview with the detective was postponed.

At school, the other girls were ready to gather around Agata, to offer their condolences and care. But she didn't come back.

The Israeli government was honoured to welcome Ezra and Agata to their new permanent residence in Tel Aviv and when extradition requests came up, as they did from time to time, they protected him from them. Agata was adrift awhile, in search of a friendship group, until she found the Trance scene. It was the first thing since self-starvation that took her out of her spiralling anxieties and made her feel free. All body, no thought.

Though they'd only been best friends for a very short while, Faith was crushed when Agata didn't come back. She came to Gail in tears, having tried to text Agata and finding the number disconnected. She asked if she might visit her flat after school one day. Gail thought about what had passed between them the last time they'd tried to be friends. It hadn't worked out then, it wouldn't now.

The new school building, built with Ezra's donation to carry his name in his glorious lifetime, was made more significant by Melody's death. On the day of its dedication, the girls said assembly prayers for Melody and the family. Then it ended and Gail had a meeting to go to.

The headmistress called them back in to see her on the very last day of winter term. It was a different time of day from the first session they'd been summoned to. There was no sound of hockey beyond the window. The whole school was eerily quiet on this, their third and final meeting of the year.

'Well,' the headmistress said, clapping her hands together. But if it were to denote the beginning of a performance, it was she who performed, smiling tightly: 'I think there's enough improvement for us to say that Gail's place is assured here.'

Mother and daughter looked at each other, bewildered.

The headmistress clapped her hands again, a diminishing return. Was it like someone trying to turn on a robotic pet? An overhead lighting system? A woman trying to keep rhythm in her head, or to instigate a group feeling? Her pale lashes seemed to glow with misinformation as she insisted, 'Everything's gone really well since we last met, we think.'

It was almost like someone had spoken to her, had told her to keep Gail's spot at St Saviour's assured. They both looked at the headmistress like she was mad. And

Gail, seeing the name beyond the window, understood and said: 'I don't want it.'

The headmistress shifted in her seat.

'But, Gail? There's only one year to get through. For both of us.'

'I just don't think we're a good match,' explained Gail, 'I'm sorry.'

Then she slowly unhooked her long skirt at the side zip. The older women did not make a move because they could not make sense yet of what they were watching. They both sat, mesmerised.

Gail lay on the faded oriental rug in front of the head-mistress's desk and wiggled her way out of her long school skirt. The headmistress would be haunted by the vision for the rest of her life, would think of it in her most private moments, just as Gail thought of Ezra dabbing her eyes with the towel.

Underneath, Gail had on the pair of calf-length pedal pushers that Melody had bought her on her laptop when she was high. She stood up, so that they could properly see the line her body made in them. Finally, one of them found their voice.

'But those don't suit you,' said Dar, dumbly. This made Gail smile. It felt so good to smile, for real, not to please someone or to entice them or to soothe them.

'Mum. I'm seventeen now. I can get away with anything.'

Gail carefully folded the skirt and handed it to the headmistress, leaning across the desk. Dar was wrong: the pedal pushers looked great.

'Frame this skirt,' Gail incanted. 'Put it with the sports trophies in the hallway so everyone can know I was once a student here. It will be a selling point when prospective parents come to tour.'

The headmistress couldn't speak.

'I wish you *all* the luck in the world!' Gail trilled.

Dar stood up. Gail held the door for her. Then she put her arm through her mother's as they walked down the hall and out towards the exit. Her mother was surprised to still be touched by this gesture of closeness, and leaned into it, inhaling her scent, recognising it as almost, but not quite, her own.

They passed Ezra's name for the last time, hanging over the new building, girls entering and exiting him in his honour.

Out in the world the sun was bright and made the December cold feel like a splash in the face. As they walked towards the park, they both turned their eyes from the newspaper stands. There was never any good news.

'But where are you going to finish school?'

'I'm done with school now.' Gail smiled.

'But . . . but what will become of you?' Dar almost said, 'What will become of us,' but she caught it just in time.

Gail persuaded her mother to head home without her, that she'd meet her back at the flat. She'd walked her to the bus stop, watched her climb up to the top deck, where dreams are made and obscenities shrieked. Then she turned and walked up the path until it turned into the wrought-iron gates of the Parliament Hill entrance.

The Cartier watch on her wrist was something she could now symbolically bury in the wildest corner of the Heath, telling the universe she was offering it up as an exchange, that she was walking away from being disturbed. She scoped the perfect place to conjure this spell.

However, the day after she'd been gifted it, she'd had the watch valued, and Terry Loft had been right: it was worth 25K. And she decided that the more evolved way to leave behind the chaos she'd come from was to keep it close, until it was time to sell. All refugees who ever sewed rubies into the hems of their skirts know this, as, on a cellular level, do their descendants.

Faith may or may not have stood at a top window of St Saviour's and watched as Gail entered the park. It really didn't matter to Gail. The pedal pushers accentuated her ass, which was round, high and firm and wouldn't always be that way – would, through the years, take on a different shape and texture, because that's what happens to teenage girls if they stay alive.

As for Ezra Levy? Once he boarded the jet to Tel Aviv he never looked back. He missed Melody until the day he died and tried to pretend he hadn't seen her that way the final time. As penance, he pulled some strings so that her final dress, on which she'd worked so hard all those nights he'd turned her away, was placed on display in the V&A's permanent collection. Having been something of a father figure to the boy, he covered Loft's medical bills for the rest of his life. But he never set foot in England again. Or if he did, no one, not the general public or the government, and certainly not Gail Susa, ever found out about it.

CHAPTER 37

Two letters came for Gail on Christmas Eve. The one from Dar had taken the entirety of her stay at the Levy house to write and she'd kept working on it when she was back. She knew it would come with today's afternoon post and that she'd be at the hospital, that Gail would have the space and privacy to read it alone.

My baby,

I love you so much. You're the only thing other than the full moon that makes me exclaim, 'Wow!' when I pass around a corner and see it unexpectedly. I know I get things wrong. I know I need too much from you. There's a lot of stuff, believe it or not, that I try to keep from you. I know you're more brilliant than I am. I know you're more troubled than I am. What I mean is, I know the world troubles you more. Because I see a way to solve things. And I march and shout, and I see you and it all just sits in you. I know you think nothing can be solved. I fix things at work, I fix broken bones, I watch people heal. But I watch them die too. I'm so sorry for letting you down. I am so, so ashamed. I don't know how to love you less. We are each other. I carried you for nine months. But I don't want you to carry me for a lifetime. I didn't know I was doing it. You can be so cruel. But I set that up: I'm the only one here for you to be cruel to. Testing out your powers. I want to say, 'I can take it.' Sometimes I don't know if I can. But you're not my abuser. You're just a confused teenage girl. I'm sorry if I let your power scare you. It scared me too. I'm going to get better at this.

And I'll love you always,
Mum

But Gail didn't open it because she saw the other envelope first and it took her whole attention, reassuring her that what they'd had in her head was real. Before he permanently ceased all communications, the great and troubled man with whom she'd sought to entwine himself posted Gail a letter, her palpable unravelling having weighed on his mind despite his own accelerating problems.

He did have beauty and intense vulnerability at his core despite the public 'vulgarities' and the ego. Where his dad had arrived in England from, the sense of never being British despite how big he'd made it here, how much money and power he'd accrued. She had said enough over the last six months that he saw she had no idea what she *was,* he understood the extent to which she had projected onto him. He rarely had to post his own letters but this one felt like a magic spell that needed to be done before he could reset for the new year. And so he trudged out in the snow, dodging people's eyes, despite the anxiety in the pit of his stomach that something had begun that was, for the first time ever, potentially out of his control. He went without any security.

As closely as the papers had followed the stories, most didn't recognise him with his hat pulled down. No one understood what he was really like. The woman he'd felt closest to was gone and his heart just couldn't take it any more. But rolling out with that deep lost love was the ember for this silly, crazy girl who thought she had come to know him. She'd suspected that he hated himself. And suspected that he thought he was the greatest that ever lived. Because she was that way too. She didn't know how hard it was to live this way, an entire lifetime.

He looked at the postbox, noted from the embossed symbol on the red pillar which monarch had been reigning when it had been erected. 'Ah,' he said to himself, because he was very learned despite what people knew of him, 'that postbox was an error! It says "Edward VIII" but he never took the throne.' And it pleased him. That his letter to the girl with time to save herself was going through the postbox that never should have been. The envelope, as it slipped into the red slot, felt like an unlocking and he breathed deeply, and though, by Christmas, things would be very different for him, in this moment he was glad to be forced outside by his concern for Gail and felt that the world, at this exact moment beneath this exact sky, was very beautiful.

23rd December 2016
Dear Gail,
I suppose you might not receive this until after the holidays. I just want to say, thank you for all your

letters. I know people will ask, 'Why are you trying, you're only a teenager?' But I was only a teenager and I ruled the world. I'm not scared of you but a lot of people will be. I understand you were only trying to help me. You can stop now.
    Love
    George

Acknowledgements

Thank you to my parents, to Lucia Zazarro, and to Sophie Heawood, who all offered childcare so I could finish this book. To CJ: YES, you're my favourite!

. . . though my sister, Lisa, is my first call on matters major or minor and gave me the seed of inspiration for this story.

My mum also seeded something by recording *Pretty Poison* and *Theorem* off the TV and showing them to me when I was probably too young, so they could percolate all these years. I treasure this about you.

Shana Feste (and Brian Kavanaugh-Jones and Ellis, Waylon and Odessa), getting to stay with you was the highlight of the year.

S.B. and Maysan, thank you for making sure we are always digitally connected, can all be together occasionally, and for driving me to buy my mother stick-on cannabis patches when we are.

Sara Pascoe – this book made it to the end because of your support.

Nikkie Eager – you know what you did and what it means to me.

My gratitude to Eva Wiseman and Jonathan Coe for the very early reads and encouragement.

Lorraine Kirke, thank you for letting me ask so many questions.

Maayan Zilberman: my voice of reason, my soul sister, thank G-d for you.

Nick Hornby, there's so much to thank you for, I wouldn't know where to begin (and you'd tell me if I started in the wrong place or if I, e.g. named a footballer *Terry*).

David Greer – for your expertise, kindness and generosity.

David Austin and Lucie Avery, for helping me to get the lyrics cleared.

Ilona Jasiewicsz for the catches in the copy-edit.

Lettice Franklin, my superb editor, working on these last two books with you has been the best experience of my career. Thank you to Clarissa Sutherland, Sian Baldwin, Jenny Lord and everyone at Weidenfeld who's been excited about what we've done.

To Felicity Rubinstein, Elinor Burns and now Ariel Meislin, true believers, all. It sounds weird saying 'you believe in me' like there are sceptics who aren't sure you exist, but when you're a writer for a living, it can feel that way.